ᗰEAR ᗰMERICA

The Second Diary of Abigail Jane Stewart

Cannons at Dawn

KRISTIANA GREGORY

SCHOLASTIC INC. • NEW YORK

Library of Congress Cataloging-in-Publication Data

Gregory, Kristiana.
Cannons at dawn : the second diary of Abigail Jane Stewart /
Kristiana Gregory. — 1st ed.
p. cm. — (Dear America)
Sequel to: The winter of red snow.
Summary: From the winter of 1779 until 1781, Abigail Stewart and her family
follow the path of her father's Continental Army unit after their Valley Forge
home burns down, enduring harsh winters and scarce food, and narrowly
escaping danger time and again.

Trade Paper-Over-Board edition ISBN 978-0-545-21319-6
Reinforced Library edition ISBN 978-0-545-28088-4

1. United States—History—Revolution, 1775–1783—Juvenile fiction.
[1. United States—History—Revolution, 1775–1783—Fiction. 2. Diaries—
Fiction.] I. Title.
PZ7.G8619Can 2011
[Fic]—dc22
2010032431

10 9 8 7 6 5 4 3 2 1   11 12 13 14 15

The text type was set in ITC Legacy Serif.
The display type was set in Dear Sarah.
Book design by Kevin Callahan

Printed in the U.S.A.   23
First edition, May 2011

Cannons at Dawn is dedicated to my wonderful mother, Jeanne Kern Gregory, whose ancestors marched with General Washington and were from Kernstown, Virginia. Mom's love for writing, reading, and research inspired me as a young child and inspires me still.

Also, this is in loving memory of Ann Reit, my longtime editor — a formidable and often terrifying one — who guided me through The Winter of Red Snow. It was great fun brainstorming with her and we became dear friends. About writer's block she said, "Forget about it. Just tell the story!" I miss her deeply.

Valley Forge,
Pennsylvania

1779

January 2, 1779, Saturday, morning

"Abby, when will Papa come back home?" Sally asked again. Though she is seven, she understands naught about war and she asks this question every morning. She is poking the coals for breakfast and holding back her long apron, careful that it doesn't catch fire like last winter.

"Papa will come home when General Washington says so," I answered. I sit by the hearth so my little ink jug will keep thawing. It is freezing from last night and snowing again. Gusts of wind rattle our windows.

Elisabeth just came in from the barn, eggs in her apron. Snow covers her cap and even the strings tied under her chin. Beth is the eldest of us three sisters. She smiles to see me writing in my journal. We both know that any moment our mother will turn from the fire and see that I am not frying the pork as I should be.

"Abigail, dear," Mama said, right on schedule. "Time to rest thy quill. The skillet is ready. You are twelve and should know this by the good smell of butter and onions in the pan."

"Yes, Mama," I said. She has picked up Johnny from his cradle and is drying his bottom with the hem of her skirt. Her eye is on me, but she is smiling.

Before bed

A full moon has broken through the clouds. It is so bright, this table by the window needs no candle. Elisabeth is opposite me, writing another letter to Ben Valentine. He has asked for the pleasure of her company in the hospital while his wounds heal, but Philadelphia is eighteen miles by snowy road. She fancies this soldier. As her quill moves over the paper I pretend not to look, but I *am* looking. I squint, hoping to see a love word.

"Abigail," she whispered. "You'll hurt thy neck staring."

"Beth, what say you to Mr. Valentine? How far up did the doctors cut off his arm?"

"Hush, Abby. We'll wake Mama." She glanced toward the bed we share with our mother.

Sally was asleep in her trundle, Johnny in his

cradle, though soon he shall be too big for it, as he has passed his first birthday. When Papa joined the Army a few weeks ago, we closed the upper room to save heat and now all of us sleep here by the fire. Even so, by morning our water bucket has ice.

We worry about him being a soldier. This war has gone on for nearly four years. My father is a cobbler. He is not young.

"A man needs to stand up for his country," he told us before walking down the lane with neighbours who were also joining the Continental Army. They each carried a hunting rifle and rolled-up blanket. The morning was cold with a light snowfall. I wished Papa had waved to us before the road turned, but I saw only the tuft of his queue and snow gathering on the back of his shirt.

Now he is camped with Washington's main Army in New Jersey and our enemies are wintering in the fine houses of New York, the city. The British will grow fat there, I hope, and be too merry for war. I hate them. I want them to sail back to

England and leave us alone. We have declared our independence from King George III, but still they fight us.

Elisabeth is sprinkling sand on her page to dry the ink, now I shall do the same. We are both yawning this late hour. The night is lovely, the fields aglow from the moon, but the wind is fierce. Sparks are blowing down our chimney onto the rug —

Days later

Philadelphia. My throat is sore from crying. Our pretty little house in Valley Forge is gone!

I am writing this by an attic window in Philadelphia. We arrived by sleigh a few days ago, distraught and unbelieving.

That terrible night Elisabeth and I tried to stomp out the burning rug — holding high our hems so our skirts wouldn't catch — but flames jumped to a curtain. We screamed for Mama. She scooped up Johnny and pulled Sally awake. Beth grabbed blankets. I swept all from our table into a basket: a bowl of walnuts and our writing things.

When we opened the door to run out, wind fueled the fire with a hot *swoosh*.

There was no time for us to draw water from the well. Neighbours came running with buckets, but there was naught they could do.

We stood barefoot in the snow, shivering, while flames hissed out the windows then brought down the walls. Sparks flew to the barn. It flared like a torch. When we heard the helpless shriek of Buttercup, our faithful old mare, Elisabeth and I ran to pull open the door. Our chickens squawked and there was one long *moo* from Brownie as they fled out into the cold night.

Though our animals are safe with neighbours, I am still teary writing this.

To continue . . .

We are not with relatives as we had hoped. How weary we are from having walked in the cold — three long days — looking for my uncles, who live here in Philadelphia. At night we took shelter in a stable, warmed by burrowing in hay. Our only clue to our uncles' where-abouts came from a shopkeeper sweeping snow off his step, who knew them. He said that when the British occupied this city last winter, they ransacked and burned many houses. My uncles and their families moved away, but where, he did not know. It seems the enemy destroyed their letters to us.

"Those swine Englishmen," said the shopkeeper. He spit in the icy gutter. "Now they have taken New York City. How many Patriots there have been forced from their homes, God only knows."

On our fourth day of wandering and being so very hungry, a lady kind in heart and deed saw us in the street. Actually, she heard Johnny yowling from Mama's cloak, and invited us into her tiny cottage. Her name is Mrs. Darling.

The five of us have made a cozy bed in her attic, with the blankets Elisabeth rescued. I am awake as an owl; Mother, too. I can see firelight through cracks in the floorboards and feel some warmth from the stone chimney. Still it is cold. My breath makes frost.

"Can you not sleep, Abby?" Mama just whispered.

"Not yet, Mother."

"Then mind thy candle, dear."

"Yes, Mama." I am careful with fire. I always lick my thumb and finger to pinch the flame so a draft will not relight it.

Where was I? Oh yes. The night of the fire, our neighbours, the Doogans, took us in. Then the next morning friends came to console us. They brought shoes, a cloak for each of us, a kettle, some spoons, also a basket with figs, apples, and beef pies. All offered us shelter, but Mama thought it best to be with Papa's brothers in Philadelphia.

Our farewells were tearful.

Without a house and without Papa to build one, would we ever return?

Mr. Doogan helped us into his sleigh, set warm bricks at our feet, and covered us with quilts. He whistled to the horses then drove out of Valley Forge. The countryside was white save for the smoldering black ruins of our home.

Mama was silent.

Walnut Street, Philadelphia

Am in the attic this afternoon, hunched into a blanket. I scratched ice off the window to look out at the street below. A boy has just stepped from the wigmaker's shop carrying a tall box. Though it is sunny, I can see frost from his breath. He wears the short apron of an apprentice and appears to be on an errand. Does he live in a warm house, I wonder? Is his Papa at war, too?

I miss my friends Lucy, Molly, Naomi, and Ruth. But when I think of them, I remember the fire. It haunts me how swiftly the curtains burned, how the roof caved in with a dreadful, hissing crash.

I cannot stop thinking about that night.

Am not sure of the date

When Mrs. Darling invited us in, we were astonished to see our dear friends Helen Kern and baby Olivia! They arrived two weeks ago, after bidding us farewell in Valley Forge. When we told her about the fire, Helen's eyes filled with tears.

"Your lovely home is gone?" she asked.

At this Sally burst out, "I miss Buttercup."
She sobbed. "And Pinny-Pin, my chicken."

"Oh dear . . . dear."

I felt heartsore to hear Sally cry so.

"Papa will build us a new house, Sally," said
I. "A new house with a new barn. We'll get our
animals back—"

"But first the war must end," she wailed. "How
long will that be?"

Helen's face went pale. Her husband died last
winter at Valley Forge. She is only sixteen. We
looked over at Mrs. Darling pouring tea into cups
but neither did she answer Sally. Her husband is
camped with the Army, same as Papa.

Mama went to a bench by the hearth then
pulled my sister into her lap. Big as Sally is, my
mother rocked her and rocked her.

Beth and I squeezed hands. We kept our
tears quiet.

Later

The lamplighter has just come up the street with
his ladder and jug of whale oil. These tall lamps

are lit every night. I miss the darkness of Valley Forge and being able to see stars. I miss being there with Papa. He was always the last one to bed and knew how to stoke the coals so they would keep us warm through the cold night.

Papa made us feel safe.

Alas, Helen Kern also has suffered disappointment. Her cousins sent a letter inviting her for Christmas—which was why she left our home—but when she arrived in Philadelphia her cousins' house was boarded up. She could not get in. Neighbours knew naught of the family's whereabouts. After hours of wandering, Helen met Mrs. Darling coming out of a bakery.

Now, once again we are all living under the same roof.

January 12, 1779, Tuesday

This morning, Sisters and I went out for fresh air. While crossing the street on the raised stepping-stones, three soldiers on horseback rode by. One sat taller than the others. His great cloak draped down over his saddle to the top of his boots.

General George Washington!

We had seen him many times last winter in Valley Forge when our family brought his clean laundry to Headquarters. The two men with him today wore blue coats with the shoulder patches of officers.

Elisabeth was so surprised, she pointed. "What is the Commander in Chief doing here?" she asked. "Is not his Army camped in New Jersey?"

Sally tried to run after the horsemen as they rounded the corner, but she slipped and fell, soaking her skirt in an icy puddle. Beth and I helped her up.

"Sally, you cannot chase Mr. Washington," I said.

"But what if Papa came with him? Maybe Mama's letter reached him and he is searching for us."

Beth and I looked at each other. Our mother has not sent a letter. Each time she sits at the table to write, she dips the quill into the ink and pens two words: "Dearest husband," but that is all. Then she crumples the letter into the fire.

I did not tell Sally this.

Sisters and I stepped along the sunny side of the street where snow had melted and the cobblestones were not as icy. We could see the General and his two officers dismount in front of an elegant brick home and go inside. A Negro footman led the horses to a stable.

Sally hurried to the door, but just as she reached for the brass knocker, I grabbed her arm. "We must not intrude," I said.

"But General Washington knows us. We can ask about Papa."

"Not now," said Elisabeth with a glance my way. She and I have agreed that at times our little sister is too curious so it is best to keep her busy. "Sally, let us do a good deed and visit the hospital."

And so, to keep from slipping, the three of us took hands, then rounded the corner.

Evening, still Tuesday

As soon as Sisters and I rushed in through Mrs. Darling's door, we chattered about seeing the General. Mrs. Darling was at the hearth plucking a goose. She blew a feather away from her face then said, "He and his wife are old friends of mine. They are staying at the home of Henry Laurens, who used to be President of Congress."

"Lady Washington is here, *too*?" I cried.

"Yes, dear. This winter has been so mild, Congress invited the Commander in Chief to make Philadelphia his Headquarters. He and Martha have been here since before Christmas, many officers and their wives as well. Lord Stirling has been left in charge of the encampment."

We smiled upon hearing Lady Washington's name. She was generous and kind to us last winter. The laced handkerchiefs she gave us were saved from our fire only because we each had the habit of carrying one tucked in a sleeve.

I pondered a way to see her, to say hello again. A lady such as herself could tell us truly about the soldiers, if they were better fed and warmer than last year.

Also, I pondered our visit to the hospital. The Battle of Monmouth was six months ago yet Ben Valentine was still fevered. One arm was a stump of bloody bandages. When Elisabeth spoke his name, he opened his eyes but was too weak to lift his head.

"I write his letters for him," said a lady sitting by another cot. Her dress was brown, her apron snow-white. The black feather pinned over her heart told us two things: that she was a widow and that she was a Patriot. Black cloth comes from England, thus women in mourning refuse to sew gowns of this color.

Elisabeth wants to return to the hospital, but I do not. It stank of wet wool and vinegar. The rats running underneath the beds were big as puppies.

January 13, 1779, Wednesday
You would not guess our country is at war by the gaiety in Philadelphia. I am writing at Mrs.

Darling's desk, by a tall front window. Three fine carriages have just rolled by, splashing through the wet snow. A dance is to be held at Mrs. Powell's within the hour.

Mrs. Darling was invited to the party, but she burned her hand yesterday when the kettle spilled. She has asked me to deliver a cake in her stead. Oh, the aroma of baked apples and cinnamon! Would it be wretched if I pinched off a crispy corner to taste?

Elisabeth is at the hospital, reading *Gulliver's Travels* to Ben. He has been cheered by seeing her. This morning after she and I cleaned breakfast dishes, she went to the frosted windows and wrote with her finger: first, "Mr. and Mrs. Benjamin Valentine," then "Elisabeth Ann Valentine." I think she has made up her mind about a husband.

Evening

Sally walked with me to Mrs. Powell's, three streets toward the river. A servant girl my age showed us upstairs to a ballroom, where ladies and gentlemen were dancing a cotillion. Such beautiful gowns swishing about the floor! The men wore buff and blue coats, and their breeches were tied at the knee with a bow. I believe their white stockings were silk, and the buckles on their shoes, silver.

When a fiddler began playing a march, I realized Sally was no longer at my side. I held my breath. Where had she gone? Soon enough I spied her with a group of ladies—all familiar to me from last winter—and Mrs. Washington! Such was my haste to reach them I near dropped my basket with the cake.

"Pardon us, Lady Washington," I said. "Please forgive our intrusion."

"Dear girls, 'tis lovely to see you again. How fares your mother?"

Then in a tumble of words, Sally told about the fire and how Papa joined the army. "Have you seen him, ma'am?"

Mrs. Washington was my height and plump as a pretty hen. There was color in her cheeks and her eyes were kind. She took Sally's hand. "I am sorry about your house, dear child, and that you miss your father. Try not to worry."

Then turning to me she said, "Abby, perhaps you know that families such as yours are encamped with the soldiers? Many are those who fled the city of New York because they lost their homes to the British. 'Tis a rough life, I assure you. And my husband says that women and children are troublesome for the Army."

She leaned close to whisper. "However, dear, I do think they bring comfort to the men."

"Thank you, Mrs. Washington." I dipped a quick curtsy then tugged Sally's apron.

Downstairs at the door, I remembered to hand my basket to the young servant. She lifted the cloth then gave me a sly smile. "Aye, girl," she said in a heavy Scottish brogue, "the very same happens to my cakes. One corner always disappears."

January 15, 1779, Friday, before bed

Mama and Helen Kern are nursing their babies by the fire while my Sisters play dominoes at the table. Mrs. Darling has been reading aloud to us from the *Evening Post*. Her rocker creaks like the slow ticking of a clock.

I shall never forget last evening. The ballroom was in the most elegant home I have ever seen. Chandeliers sparkled with so many candles and there was a wall of mirrors. The music and the swishing of dresses and the *clip-step-clip* of shoes on the polished wood floor will stay with me always. As Sally and I were leaving, we noticed General Washington speaking with officers. He stands a head taller than most — six-feet-two inches, some say. I recognized one of the generals from last winter: Benedict Arnold. He was hoisting a glass of punch and seemed quite jolly. He still limps badly from his wound at Saratoga.

I should not have stared, but I did — just for a moment — from under the lace of my cap. I am *certain* that one of Benedict Arnold's legs is shorter than the other. His boot heels were uneven.

Lady Washington's words have stayed with me. If families bring comfort to soldiers, might we do the same for Papa?

After an argument with Mother

This time in the attic, I am most unhappy. And cold. My fingers are stiff holding this quill.

When I asked Mama if we might join the Army, she said, "The Army is no place for a baby learning to walk. 'Tis too dangerous. I fear something would happen to our Johnny."

My parents still grieve over the five tiny gravestones in Valley Forge. Johnny is the only one of my six brothers to have lived through his first winter. Now this is his second winter. I reminded Mama of this, and how he is a fine, healthy baby, but she pointed me up the ladder. I should not have stomped my foot at her or raised my voice.

But I did, thus here I am until supper.

January 17, 1779, Sunday

Sometimes it seems that all goes wrong.

I have enjoyed helping Mrs. Darling prepare our evening meals, but a few days ago I broke the crane in her fireplace. The iron arm snapped in two when I hooked a pot of beans onto it. The pot fell into the coals, scattering ashes and spilling all that we had soaked overnight. Thus, instead of pork and beans for three nights' supper, we ate bread and butter with pickles.

Then yesterday when everyone was out visiting a neighbour, I decided to make tea for when they returned. I opened our door to scoop fresh snow into a bucket. Behind me on the table was a ham. I had just brushed it with honey and poked it with cloves, readying it for the spit. But while I was outside, a shaggy, muddy dog trotted up to me. He was wagging his tail and had a certain confidence about him. He licked my hand, then went straight into the house. At the table, he stood on his hind legs, snatched the ham, and quick as a flea, he was gone.

I was too surprised to yell at him.

Mrs. Darling did not fault me for these dreadful losses. The crane had rusted, she said, thus was weak. Blacksmith Campbell repaired it, then set it safely into the hearth. As for the dog who stole our ham, it seems that he, too, is an old friend of Mrs. Darling's.

"I call him Captain Lost Boy," she told us. "He comes by now and then for a good meal. I enjoy his company. Sometimes he stays all evening by the fire."

The other mishap was this morning at Christ Church. After three hours of sitting terribly still and trying to listen to Reverend Fogg, I yawned. I could not help myself. It was loud as a belch, and many turned to look at me. A boy even stuck out his tongue and pointed. Wanting to disappear, I sunk low into my cloak. In the pew across from us were Lady Washington and the General. He was facing forward and gave no indication he had heard me. But dear Mrs. Washington glanced over at me with the tiniest of smiles. I am most fond of her.

I feel somewhat better having written all this tonight.

January 23, 1779, Saturday

Days have passed since I opened my diary. We have all been ailing with heavy colds and still my throat is sore, but not Johnny. He is most vigorous.

"See how he stands up by himself?" I showed Mama as he held on to my finger. In his frock and chin-cap, his pink baby feet took one step then another along the braided rug.

"He is a big boy now," Mama agreed, setting down a letter from Papa. A neighbour from Valley Forge delivered it this morning after searching for us. Papa wrote that he is in Middlebrook, New Jersey, with the 2nd Pennsylvania Brigade.

Mama watched Johnny take another step with me. Her brow furrowed. "Hmm," she said. "Middlebrook. My cousin Deborah lives in the village there, with her husband, James, and five — or is it now six? — children. We last exchanged letters before Christmas. She has invited us often."

"Oh Mother, let us go visit," I said.

She did not answer, but I noticed a slight sparkle in her eye.

Next evening

Captain Lost Boy came for supper tonight. Sally tied a leather strap around his neck for a collar. This time he ate from a bowl, then he curled up by the hearth to sleep. He was such a tired dog, he was not roused when Johnny lay at his side and stroked his furry ear.

January 25, 1779, Monday

At long last Mama has written a letter to Papa. Sisters and I leaned over the table as she read it aloud. ". . . and do not worry about us, Edward. Though we have lost our home, we are together. And soon we shall be near you, staying with cousins. You remember Deborah's bright red hair—"

Upon hearing that we would indeed winter near Papa, Sally and I hugged Mama, then hugged her again. But Elisabeth stood back. She is dark-eyed and as pretty as our mother.

"Mother?" she said. Her voice trembled. "May I have your blessing to remain in Philadelphia? Helen and I want to help in the hospital. Our soldiers need care — Ben Valentine especially — and Mrs. Darling has invited us to live with her."

Mama's eyes grew moist. She touched my sister's cheek then nodded.

Last night in bed I could not help my tears. Elisabeth leaned on her elbow and gave me a tender look. "Abby," she whispered. "You will be the eldest now. Please stop arguing with Mama. It grieves her so, and she needs your help to look after Sally and Johnny. Papa shall be very proud of you."

I burrowed under our quilt. Beth is my best friend. I get stomachaches worrying about Johnny. And I never know what Sally might do or say. If anything happens to them, I would come undone.

Monday after supper, looking at maps and an almanac

Middlebrook is several days north, up the Delaware River. Ice is along the banks. We shall sail as far as possible, then walk the rest of the way. If more snow falls, I do not know what we will do for shelter. We have no money for an inn or tavern.

Mrs. Darling tried to cheer us. She explained that next Saturday is a full moon, the second one this month.

"'Tis a good omen for travel, Mrs. Stewart," she

said to encourage Mama. "Two moons in January are rare."

Mr. Campbell's family will go with us. He says the Army needs another blacksmith, and by coincidence his son is in the same brigade as Papa. Mr. Campbell also said the soldiers have built huts in which to stay warm, but he does not know about the others — the blacksmiths such as himself, cobblers, wheelwrights, and the wagon drivers who haul the cannons.

"Perhaps we will live in tents," he told us with a questioning glance toward his wife.

It is selfish of me, but I am thankful Papa has a hut, and the rest of our family shall be cozy in a cousin's home. If Mrs. Campbell is unhappy about tenting in the snow, she is bearing up well. She patted Mama's hand as if to say, *Not to worry, all shall be fine.*

Our belongings are few: a kettle, small sacks of flour and dried beef, a blanket each, and of course Mama's long, wooden spoon. My diary, pen, and packets of ink powder fit into the pocket tied under my skirt — a cork will keep my little jug from spilling.

How I wish Elisabeth had not been crying when we said our farewells. She pulled her apron up over her face. My throat gets tight not knowing how long we'll be apart.

Aboard the Little Liberty

Late afternoon. We are sitting on deck, huddled together for warmth near the mainmast. Tarps cover bundles of supplies for various villages and there are barrels of salted fish roped together. Mr. Campbell's mule and wagon are in the stern. We have just eaten our supper: some small apples and beef pies that Mrs. Darling packed for us this morning.

The sky is white with falling snow (thus the splotches on this page). Mama has spread her cloak like wings over Johnny and Sally to keep them dry. Her face is pale. If I could see *my* face, I would say it is fretting, and that my whole self is shivery. The wind is cold. Chunks of ice are in the water as we glide past the frozen banks. I do believe winter is the most dreadful time to travel.

We have come to a narrow stretch of river

where there are soldiers on shore. When I saw their bayonets, I thought they were our Continentals. But now I realize their coats are crimson, and they are cursing at us!

"Rebels . . . traitors!" they keep yelling. "Drop your anchor! By order of His Majesty, King George of England, halt!" Then shots rang out. We could hear the *thump-thump-thump* of musket balls hitting the hull. Splinters flew in the air.

A murmur passed among those of us crouched on deck trying to hide. Sally stood up to look over the side, but I pulled her down. This scared her and she flung herself on Mama.

"What will happen if the ship stops?" Sally cried.

Mr. Campbell did not give Mama or me a chance to make up a pretty answer. He said, "Those Redcoats will hang us. Or they will shoot us."

Mother gave him a worried look. "I thought the Delaware was safe," she said.

"Nothing is safe, Mrs. Stewart. The Redcoats are everywhere. Their generals are moving troops through our colonies as if playing on a giant chessboard."

Mr. Campbell pointed over the bow, toward the trees. "British patrols from New York have been watching this ship, of that I am certain. And they shall track us all the way to Middlebrook, just to harass us."

Sally buried her head in Mama's cloak.

I must put away this pen, my hand trembles so.

Somewhere along the Delaware

I am sick with dread, having seen our enemies and knowing they are still in the woods. Darkness has fallen. We are in a tavern, warming up. It is about ten o'clock.

Back to our voyage: By a miracle, a stiff wind filled our sails and our captain steered us fast away. The Redcoats still fired at us. Even in the falling snow I could see smoke from their guns and smell their powder. An older man among us was wounded in the arm. The soldiers chased along the shore until an island came between us, then they dropped from sight. Still we could hear their shouts in the forest.

When the river ice became too thick for

Little Liberty, her crew unloaded the equipment and passengers — there were about twenty of us headed to different villages — then turned back for Philadelphia. By this time it had stopped snowing and the clouds opened like a curtain to show us the moon, filling the sky with light. We did not argue with Mr. Campbell when he said we must hurry to put distance between those soldiers and us.

After some miles, chilled and hungry, we spied a tavern and stopped. It was crowded and noisy despite the late hour. Mr. Campbell peeked in a window to make sure there were no British.

"My husband was killed in the Battle of Brandywine," the owner told us, pulling open her barn door for us. "Fresh hay for thy horse. Hide thy wagon here. A blacksmith on the road to General Washington's camp — that, sir, is an easy target. If the Brits don't molest ye, the cowboys shall — those are the raiders attached to no army. Dirty, filthy pirates is what I call 'em."

After serving us bread and hot onion soup, the lady showed us to a ladder nailed against the back wall. She pointed to the ceiling. We climbed up through a small opening, under the low rafters of her attic, and shut the trapdoor. It is here that I am writing by the candle she gave us. There are no windows or furniture, merely a bare floor with squash and pumpkins stored where the roof slopes down. We must stoop to move about, else bump our heads on the beams.

Our blankets are warming against the chimney.

In payment for our meal and our night's stay, Mr. Campbell will carry in firewood tomorrow morning, and we ladies will scrub this floor. I shall be glad to do so. It is muddy and stinks of urine, from past sojourners I suspect. Through the cracks I can see men downstairs eating at a long table by the fire. Their jokes are crude.

I am most thankful those rough men cannot see us.

The tavern door has just banged open . . . soldiers!

Hiding

We can scarce breathe. The Campbells, Mama, Sally, and I are lying on the floor on our bellies, each with an eye looking down through a crack. Five Redcoats are singing and tottering. Our lady made them stack their bayonets in a corner, and she is ladling soup into bowls for them. I can see the top of her cap and her aproned hips as she moves about the table. She has not looked up at the ceiling.

My candle is a puddle of wax, not giving much light. Still I have set it inside our kettle so that no one below sees its flicker.

Johnny has started to fuss! Quick, Mama is nursing him. Thank heaven the soldiers can hear naught but their own singing. Oh, when will they leave?!

Morning at the tavern

Still in the attic. Below us by the hearth, the five Brits sleep. The other men must have left in the wee hours of the night. Sunshine is coming in by the table where the widow is kneading bread. Now she kicks the soldiers' boots. "Up with ye. Up!" she yells. "Get out and about thy dirty business. Three shillings apiece, now!"

After scrubbing the attic

Finally the soldiers are gone. The lady is furious they left without paying and even more furious they stole a cooked ham from her table. They are no better than stray dogs. At least Captain Lost Boy provides friendship.

This past hour, Mr. Campbell filled one wall of the tavern with firewood, then stacked more outside under the eaves. Mother and I carried out the bucket of wash water to pour into the snow. I have a few moments with my diary while the Campbells ready their horse and wagon.

The widow has set breakfast on the table for us: porridge and stewed apples, toasted bread with butter. Tea, as well, from her summer garden. Not British tea.

"Fill thy bellies," she tells us. "Middlebrook is a long day's journey. I pray the cowboys leave ye be."

The six of us are seated now with the lady. She has asked Mr. Campbell to pray for all of us.

Following the
Continental Army

1779

Mid-March 1779

Middlebrook. Much has happened since we left Philadelphia, now several weeks past. I shall try to relate all, while Johnny naps on the ground beside me. We are on a sunny hillside looking down at Army Headquarters—a large house with shutters and a columned porch. Mrs. Washington is staying there with the General; she and I often wave to each other.

But back to our journey: The road from the tavern was snowy, but had been packed down by farmers and villagers. We kept a sharp eye, fearful of Redcoats or raiders. At last we came to a wide fork. One direction led to the encampment, the other was a narrow lane to Mama's cousin Deborah's house. The snow was too deep for Mr. Campbell's wagon, so he helped us climb out at the junction.

"'Tis but a short walk anyway," Mama said. The cottage was as she remembered from years ago. But when we knocked, the lady who opened the door had brown curls below her cap. She was not redheaded as were the five children peering out at us.

"Deborah?" Mama asked.

"No, lady. I be Suzanne. Deborah passed two months ago at Christmas; her new babe, too."

We stood in silence. Finally Mama explained why we had journeyed so far. "We have no place to call home."

"I am dreadful sorry for your loss, Mrs. Stewart. Me and James are married now. He has headaches and does not like visitors. But you folks come in by the fire before you freeze out there, the sun is going down. You can stay one night, 'tis all. I am sorry," she said again.

During a supper of biscuits and beans, James stared down at his plate. He said not a word to us or to his squirming children. Mama and I lay awake that long night. By the glow of the hearth I could see her tears. At sunrise we bade farewell to our little cousins then hiked down their lane, our blankets rolled up around our waists. Mama and I took turns carrying Johnny and our heavy iron kettle. Sally trudged behind us in the snow with our basket.

Next day

Johnny is awake now. I have given him some twigs and a pinecone to play with. To continue:

Mama led us onto the road where we had last seen the Campbells and their wagon. A forest was to our left, snowfields to our right. The air was frosty, but soon we were warmed by our brisk pace and the sun.

"Come, Daughters," Mama called. "More miles await us. We do not want to be caught out here at dark."

Sally is brave for seven years old, even holding her hem lest she trip on her skirt. But after three hours she began to lag farther and farther. We kept stopping so she could catch up. At a bend in the road I turned around to encourage her, but she had disappeared!

"Sally!" I screamed, dropping the kettle and running, slipping on ice. "Sally!" Finally I saw her by the edge of the woods. She was swinging her basket at a man reaching for her. He wore a fringed hunting shirt and a tricorn, which had fallen over his eyes in the struggle. He was laughing.

I could hear Mama running, breathing hard, Johnny on her hip, calling to us.

Just as the man grabbed Sally's skirt, two soldiers in blue rushed out from the trees. My heart pounded in terror. One of the soldiers jumped on the man, knocking him down with a punch to the jaw. The other soldier — taller and younger — pulled out a knife and held it to the fellow's neck.

"You hurt, Sally?" called the older one. How did he know my sister's name? His voice was familiar.

"Papa?" Sally and I cried at once, now recognizing his rugged face. But he waved us away.

"Go to thy mother," he ordered. Sally ran, but I disobeyed. I could not take my eyes off my father. How did he get here at this moment? He and the younger soldier removed the man's boots and slit open his shirt so it dropped to the snow. Then they made him hand over his wool stockings and breeches.

"Swine," Papa said. "My bunk mates shall make good use of your clothing, but only after we wash out the vermin. If you ever touch my family again, I shall cut your throat."

I saw only the backside of that naked man

running away through the snow, holding his hat onto his head.

Sally and I flew into Papa's arms. He hugged us for the longest time. Then he embraced our mother and hefted Johnny onto his shoulders. At first none of us spoke, but then came our questions. He introduced us to Willie, Mr. Campbell's son.

"Your letter came a few days ago," Papa told us. "I had learned that James was ill after losing Deborah and the baby. I knew he could not care for another family. My captain gave us permission to come find you. A shorter path took us through the woods where we happened to see Sally just now."

"Papa, if James is heartsore for his wife, why did he marry Suzanne?" Sally asked.

Once again, Mother and I did not have time for a pretty answer.

"James needs someone to care for his children," Papa replied. "And Suzanne needs a roof."

March 30, 1779, Tuesday

Every day I want to write in this diary, but it is trying without a quiet place to call my own. Sally or Mama or *someone* looks over my shoulder and says, "What say you, Abby girl?"

I answer by covering the page with my sleeve. I want to have secrets that no one will read!

A moment ago I stirred fresh ink powder and water into my jug, then sharpened a new quill with Mama's pen knife — alas, now Sally is asking for my help. She's trying to wash Johnny's face, but he toddled this way and is calling my name. "Babby, Babby," he cries, holding out his arms for me. That little boy makes me happy! Being the eldest is not so bad after all, though I miss Elisabeth dreadfully — the secrets we whispered, and our prayers.

Later, still Tuesday

I like Middlebrook. It's in a pretty valley with farms and meadows like Pennsylvania. There are surrounding mountains and I counted three churches with steeples. Sally plays more with Johnny, now that he can walk while holding her hand.

When Papa and Willie Campbell led us to the encampment, we were surprised to see many ladies along the edges. They were washing clothes in big kettles that hung over fires. Children seemed to be everywhere. The soldiers had built log huts for them, so they would not have to live in tents. Some women also cook and many nurse the men who are sick or who have been wounded.

We share a cabin with Mrs. Campbell, and three women from New York who lost their homes to the British. The only reason we are allowed to stay here is because we are related to a soldier. We must earn our keep. We cannot sit around and gaze at the clouds, we must launder uniforms and blankets. There is much mending of torn breeches and lost buttons. In exchange, the Army gives us rations of meat and flour.

Our hut has bunks built into the walls. A stone hearth is opposite the door and window, which has no glass. At night we cover it with an apron, so men cannot see in. After breakfast and after supper I help wipe dishes, then Sally and I take turns sweeping the dirt floor with a pine bough. For now it is home.

We have not bathed since Christmas, only washed our hands and faces. My scalp feels itchy under my cap; Sally says hers does, too.

"How long will we live here?" she asked Papa when he brought soiled shirts from his brigade for washing.

"As long as the Army is here," he answered. "When General Washington orders us to march, so will you."

"We march with the *soldiers*?"

"Behind, daughter. Far behind so none of you gets hurt in battle. You shall follow the supply wagons and cannons."

March 31, 1779, Wednesday

Today Mama told me I am thirteen years old and have been since the sixth of this month! Sally turned eight last week. We have been too busy to watch the calendar!

I looked down at my bare feet sticking out from my skirt but they do not look bigger, nor do my hands. I am older, but am I growing? I wish Elisabeth were here to tell me. There is no mirror to see if my face looks the same.

My birthday last year passed unnoticed as well. I read back in this diary to see why. We were busy in another way and my heart hurts remembering. The Fitzgerald boys fell through the ice of the Schuylkill and drowned.

I had loathed the bully, Tom, but I had not wished him dead, nor his four little brothers.

Another day, after a visit to Headquarters

I did not expect Lady Washington to invite me in when I knocked on the open door of Headquarters. Truly, it was just to deliver a message from Mama, that we would be glad to care for the General's shirts again if need be.

"Thank you for your kind offer, Abby, dear," she said. "We've hired a laundress from the village. But come to the kitchen with me, my old friend. I have a little something for you and Sally." She handed me a warm cloth. Inside were two scones with a spicy pumpkin aroma.

When she wiped her fingers on her apron, a letter that had been tucked into her waistband fell to the floor. Before she noticed, a draft blew it under a chair. I rushed over to pick it up.

"My goodness," she said. "I don't want to lose this. My son, Jacky, has written such cheerful news about my grandchildren. Thank you, Abby."

Just then a large woman in full skirts appeared, cradling an infant in her arms. She smiled and said, "Abigail, hello! I remember you from Valley Forge. You are taller this year."

"Good morning, Mrs. Knox." I stretched on my toes to see her baby's tiny pink face.

Seeing my curiosity, she said, "This is our sweet little Julia, our second daughter. 'Tis a fine spring day to be out visiting, yes? And, here comes Caty."

I curtsied to General Greene's wife, Catharine. She, too, was holding an infant. When she saw me peering at the little lace cap she said, "And this is Cornelia. She and Julia shall grow up together and be great friends."

Soon I was forgotten among the officers of many ranks coming through the central hall, boots clomping mud. Their voices were solemn. I strained to hear.

Lady Washington's Negro maid, Oney, touched my elbow. She and I had become friendly at Headquarters last winter. She said, "Abigail hon' chile, you best leave now. Mistress Wash'ton's friends are arriving for coffee. See?"

Oney nodded toward three gowned ladies coming down the hall on their way upstairs, one behind the other. Their full skirts brushed against the walls so I stepped inside a room to get out of their way. This room was crowded with officers. General Washington stood by the fire, his arm on the mantel. His hair was powdered, tied behind his neck in a queue. I saw only his profile, but noticed that his brow was furrowed.

"Our soldiers have not been paid for months!" he thundered. "Their families at home suffer and even here we have not enough food. Congress must do more to help."

Hearing this, I hid the cakes in my skirt, ashamed to have sweets and knowing other children in camp had none. The ladies now were making their rustly way up the staircase to Mrs.

Washington's parlour. As I reached the front door, a running soldier bumped into me.

"Sir," he shouted. "The Redcoats have taken Savannah. Next they shall have Charleston. They are moving through the colonies like locusts, sir."

General Washington's voice came from the room. "Where in God's name is the French fleet? We need them now!"

I stepped outside and shut the door behind me, recalling last spring in Valley Forge. Elisabeth and I had been at Headquarters fetching laundry when we overheard some officers cheering. There was great excitement because the French had just become our allies. Their army was to begin sailing across the Atlantic to help us fight the British.

Now I, too, wondered where they were. What was taking so long?

April 5, 1779, Monday

More news about the enemy. A horseman rode into camp an hour ago, yelling about a shipwreck. While transporting British troops and some of their families from Halifax to New York, the ship hit rocks and broke apart.

"One hundred forty-five Redcoats drowned," he said to cheers and hats being thrown in the air.

Mama surprised me with her boldness. She hollered, "But what happened to their wives and the little children? Did they make it to shore?"

"No, madam, they all drowned. Only some of the men survived."

I looked over at Johnny playing with stones in the dirt, and Sally tending him. I hope and pray we never sail on another ship. We do not know how to swim, and surely our heavy skirts would sink us.

Two surprises

The days are getting warmer. We see Papa now and then, but he is busy. The men drill with artillery and cannons, resulting in the same furious explosions we heard in Valley Forge. They are not in battles, but it sounds so.

More noise comes from the blacksmiths. They work over campfires by their wagons, hammering horseshoes, repairing iron chains and other metal. Cobblers, too, are hard at work, though there is not enough leather or time to keep every man in good shoes or boots. The French sent our Army handsome blue and white uniforms, but the French shoes fall apart in the mud like a lady's slipper.

Mama fears that our soldiers will be barefoot again, as they were last winter, the winter of red snow.

"Their bloody footprints made us cry," Sally reminded us.

We ladies also are busy. Behind our huts, ropes are strung between poles, for drying the many shirts and breeches and blankets on sunny days. When it rains, all is hung inside. Late this afternoon, Sally and I each carried a folded stack of laundry to Papa's camp, a mile from here along a creek.

A soldier sitting on a log was polishing his bayonet. He jumped up when he saw us. "Let me help you, ladies."

It was Willie Campbell. For the first time, I noticed his eyes are blue and gentle. He stands much taller than I remember. His knees were showing through a tear in his breeches. We gave him the laundry, then as we hurried away, I looked over my shoulder.

I was surprised to see him smiling at me. He touched the brim of his tricorn in salute.

The second surprise is that I am most eager to see him again.

June 3, 1779, Thursday

Still in Middlebrook. Parcels of mail arrived at Headquarters today. There was a letter for us from Elisabeth. While our laundry dried in the sun, we sat in the grass on the shady side of our hut. Mama began reading aloud.

"'. . . Captain Lost Boy had three puppies. *He* is a *she*. We now just call her Captain. She was so furry, we had not noticed the obvious! Every evening all of us are together in front of Mrs. Darling's fire. Captain is a good dog and makes us feel safe. . . .'"

Then Mama pressed her fingers over her mouth. "Oh," she said. Her eyes filled with tears, but she blinked them away.

"Mother, what is it?" I asked.

Mama glanced at Mrs. Campbell. "Well," she said, "Elisabeth and Ben Valentine have married and are expecting a baby."

Sally jumped up and clapped. "A baby! May we go to their wedding?"

"No wedding, Sally. Reverend Fogg has already pronounced them man and wife, and so they are. I must tell your father."

Mrs. Campbell looked up from her knitting. Her face was kind. I saw the same gentleness in her eyes that I had noticed in Willie's. She said, "Things happen fast during times such as these."

June 5, 1779, Saturday

A horseman rode into camp with news of the war:

More British ships have sailed up the Hudson, from New York Harbor—with thousands of soldiers. They seized Stony Point, the narrow part of the river where King's Ferry crosses. They have blocked the crossing and are building fortifications on the rocky cliffs. They want to draw our Patriots into an open battle.

Now General Washington has assigned one of his generals to recapture Stony Point. When I heard it shall be Anthony Wayne, my stomach swirled. General Wayne leads the Pennsylvania line — this is Papa's! And Willie Campbell's. We worry about them being in battle.

Another worry is for Mrs. Knox's baby. Julia is quite ill with fever. She is just a tiny thing, a couple of months old. Our five brothers died of fever at this age.

I wonder if Elisabeth thinks about this now that she is expecting her own child. I wish she were here so we could talk and whisper and pray.

June 7, 1779, Monday

General Washington says it's time for Lady Washington and the officers' wives to pack. They are to leave Middlebrook immediately and return to their homes.

But we who have no homes must tag behind the Army.

Word spread through camp like a blaze. "Be ready at a moment's notice, even in the middle of the night. When the soldiers move out, follow on foot. No riding in wagons allowed."

How will we do this? I look around our hut. Spoons, cups, and plates are on the hearth, a kettle simmers with tonight's soup. Mrs. Campbell's flatbread is not yet cooked. Should we roll up our blankets now?

"Abby and Sally, please get water from the creek," Mama directed. We each have a canteen, given to us by the quartermaster. It is round and made of wood with a cork for the opening. We sewed canvas straps from an old tent, and hang them on pegs in the wall. Will we remember to grab them in the middle of the dark night?

Will it be *this* night or tomorrow or the next?

On our way to Stony Point

We are resting from another day's walk in the heat. Each of us carries our blanket, canteen, and a pouch with personal things. Mama and I still take turns with our kettle — our dishes rattling under the lid — and Johnny. He is getting heavy and kicks his feet when he wants down. He is eighteen months old. If I let him walk, he runs — fast — up the road or into the trees. It scares me that he can disappear so quickly.

Mama and I are exhausted picking him up and down. I thank God this brother is so lively, but we must keep a constant eye on him.

Sally is good at keeping pace, because the baggage train is slow. Dozens of women walk in front of us and dozens behind — many also have babies on a hip, or in slings across their chests. There are small children and some girls my age, but all are busy helping their mothers.

We are a ragged, noisy crowd. Always, one child or another is wailing from hunger or from being tired. And when a little one wanders away — which is often — there is a frantic search until the child is found. On this account, I am nervous about Sally. She is curious and easily distracted.

Fortunately we have made friends with Miss Lulu and her daughter, Mazie, who is Sally's age. They are freed Negroes. Miss Lulu invited us to share her tent. It is just two tarps that she ropes between trees to make a lean-to. When it rained the other night we stayed dry except for my feet poking out in the air. We also share food and cooking. Their skillet is the scoop from a broken shovel.

Now that Sally has a friend, there are two mothers watching and calling after them.

One of the cobblers said we have crossed the border into New York. Now General Washington's Headquarters is in a tavern at New Windsor. It seems that wherever he can gather his officers and spread maps onto a table, that is Headquarters — sometimes for just a day or two.

Because he is Commander in Chief, express riders bring him reports from different parts of the colonies, about other generals and brigades. Our Continental Army is spread all the way down to the South.

Mid-June 1779

For more than a week we have been camped by a stream, while the Army keeps marching north. News comes to us as a murmur from the front line, all the way back. It is like a breeze high up in the trees, at first a quiet rustle, then loud. All of us are talking. Today, it was about one of our own spies, Captain McLane.

General Washington has ordered him to dress as a farmwife and pretend to visit her sons at Stony Point. We giggled upon hearing this, but truly, we hope he remembers two things: to shave his face and to speak in a higher voice!

All of us ladies are praying for Captain McLane.

Another hot day

Still in camp. We busy ourselves with laundry — mostly officers' uniforms — drying them over bushes and on lines strung between trees. After all is neatly folded, an orderly comes with his wagon.

"Toss thy sudsy water into the woods," the man reminded us before driving away. "Never into the river or streams. It shall be the guardhouse for any woman who soils our drinking water. By order of General Washington."

Our tent with Miss Lulu is in a thicket of pines, near a creek. To stay cool, Sally and Mazie wade in the shallows with Johnny. I watch carefully that they stay close to shore. This afternoon I was so prickly hot, I stripped down to my shift and jumped in. It was deep and cold, but I could touch the sandy bottom. It felt good to wash the dust out of my hair.

Then I helped my little sister and Mazie do the same. I held their arms while they floated in the current.

"I like this cold bath!" Mazie cried, shaking water from her pigtails.

Also to stay cool, we have made straw hats. The brims shade our faces and my eyes don't hurt so much from the sun.

June 16, 1779, Wednesday

I write this with shaking hand. Sally and I were in the woods searching for walnuts when we heard rustling. Thinking it was a deer, we stood still. I could feel something watching us. But it wasn't an animal. A figure with long, dark hair darted through the brush.

"Was that an Indian?" Sally whispered, taking my hand.

My mouth had gone dry with fear. "I think so."

When we told Mama, others began talking about the Cherry Valley Massacre last November. "Iroquois and Mohawks," a woman from New York told us.

"What happened?" Sally asked. "Did they hurt any children?"

"Hurt?" The woman laughed. Her voice was cold. "Scalped and killed. Soldiers, mothers, and their little ones. Dozens were captured, among them my own sister and her two baby daughters. We never saw them again."

We listened. The woman shook her head. "And now that Indians have joined the Redcoats, there's no safe place, not even here with the Army."

June 30, 1779, Wednesday

Steamy hot. I should like to spend an afternoon resting in the shade, but Mama needs my help. Her fingers are swollen with rheumatism so it takes two of us together to wring out each shirt, blanket, and pair of breeches. Also, I am more busy than ever with Johnny, and more anxious. He wanders away to look at sticks and bugs and squirrels. Every time I run after him, my eyes search the woods. If Indians are near, they could snatch him without a sound. I am glad that Sally has Mazie for a friend, but even those two forget to be careful. When they are playing house with sticks and stones, they often go to the edge of camp without telling us.

A few days later: good news!

Captain McLane has returned safely to Headquarters. His farm dress fooled the Redcoats. "They have not finished building their works," he reported. "Our enemy is vulnerable."

Now General Washington is planning a secret attack! These past evenings have been bright from a full moon. With his spyglass, he has been watching the British from Buckberg Mountain, and organizing his men. In the middle of the night Papa and Willie's battalion shall march with

General Wayne and hundreds more. They'll carry bayonets, but only some are allowed muskets, lest an accidental blast alert our enemy.

The terrain is rough with narrow mountain trails. No wagons with horses, no women with children will follow. We would make too much noise with our babies and clanking kettles.

We wait.

I am a selfish, worrying daughter. Papa is fighting for our freedom—for that I am deeply proud. But I want him to return unharmed. I want him to build another home for us, so we can all be together—Elisabeth, Ben, and their baby, too.

I want to have a house with doors we can lock.

Same week, more news

Our soldiers cannot build cooking fires, lest the enemy see their smoke.

"Then what does Papa eat for supper?" Sally asked.

"Perhaps pecans or walnuts from the woods," Mama replied. "There are streams everywhere. At least they have water to drink."

We learned that when our troops encounter civilians along the way, they arrest them so they will not report to the British. There are many Loyalists throughout the countryside, those loyal to King George, who would be glad to make trouble for us.

Word also is that our soldiers kill any dog they see, to keep it from barking. This so upset Sally and Mazie, they put their hands over their faces.

Sally sobbed until she had hiccups. "I wish we had one of those dogs for a friend, like Captain. I miss Papa! I miss 'Lisbeth!"

July 4, 1779, Sunday

Still we wait for news.

We have no church, but we can pray anywhere. One of the blacksmiths led all of us in the singing of Psalm 23. "The Lord is our shepherd, we shall not want. . . ." Then he gave a good sermon — short!

Today is the third anniversary of declaring our independence from King George, but we are not celebrating with cannons like last year. We move as quietly as possible through camp and keep our cooking fires low. We are miles from our soldiers, perhaps twenty, but still we do not want to draw attention to ourselves. British spies might be near. We have no weapons.

"They could capture us if they wanted," said Mrs. Campbell. She was mixing flour with drops of water in the palm of her hand. Rolling the dough into a ball, she looked over at Mama. "If they don't kill us, they will force us to wash and cook for them. Imagine how that would upset our husbands."

Mama nodded. She was at the fire, positioning a flat rock onto the coals. This is where we pat down the dough, to bake ash-cake when our kettle is full of laundry. I wondered if she was remembering how Papa charged out of the woods to save Sally.

"I worry," Mama said. "Such an act of violence against wives and children could weaken the American Army."

Sally leaned into Mama's skirt. "What if Indians kidnap us?"

I could hear Mama sigh. "Some Indians are

our friends," she said. "They are good people. They
have families like ours."

"But what about that massacre?"

Mama's gaze went up to the sky. "There is
much we do not understand, Daughter."

The summer heat is moist and heavy, even at night.
Mosquitoes swarm and bite us through the cloth
of our shifts. It is misery trying to sleep with them
buzzing in our ears. They are nasty things.

During the day between chores, children wade
in the creeks and splash one another. Sally and I
love to take Johnny by his hands and swing him
over the water, so his feet skim the cool surface.
Back and forth, up and down.

"Fly, birdie, fly!" we sing.

His laugh makes all of us laugh.

When Johnny is tired, Mazie likes to carry him
around against her shoulder, patting him until he
falls asleep. Against her black skin, he looks like
a porcelain doll. "There, there, lil' babe," she says
to him.

During moments like this I forget we are
at war.

July 17, 1779, Saturday

Word spread into camp from a horseman riding fast.

Yesterday just after midnight, the Patriots moved on Stony Point. Some chopped through the woods with axes, others waded waist deep through marshes. Providence was with the Americans! Clouds hid the moon. High winds forced the British ships to pull up their anchors and sail downriver, taking with them their rockets and cannons. Thus our enemies on shore were even more vulnerable.

In the brief battle — it lasted perhaps an hour — General Wayne was wounded in the head with a musket ball. He managed to stay in command, though, and encouraged his men to keep fighting.

Some 80 Patriots were wounded. When we heard that fifteen were killed, all of us in camp fell silent. We looked around at one another. My chest felt tight with panic. Who among us might hear terrible news? It seems there are 100 women or so, many with children and babies.

Mother, Mrs. Campbell, and Miss Lulu kneeled in the dirt by our tent. They bowed their heads, praying aloud. Several others joined them.

"Please protect our country, Lord. Protect our men."

"Have mercy on us all."

"Thy will be done, Lord."

Mazie and Sally clung to my skirt as we stood listening.

Afternoon, still waiting for news

Word continues to dribble our way.

Before our soldiers crept onto Stony Point, they were given a ration of rum to fortify themselves and a piece of white paper to pin to their hats. This was to help them in the darkness, to tell themselves apart from the enemy.

In the end, twenty Redcoats were shot or bayoneted, others drowned in the Hudson trying to escape. Hundreds more were captured and are being marched to a prison camp in Pennsylvania. Even though General Wayne was bleeding from his head wound, he was able to send word to General

Washington. The horseman repeated it to us like this:

"Sir, the fort and garrison are ours. Our men behaved like men determined to be free."

The messenger then galloped away without answering our shouted questions.

When will we know names? It is agony waiting.

July 18, 1779, Sunday

At last, news has reached camp. An express rider stayed in his saddle and read from a scrap of paper, the names of our soldiers killed at Stony Point. We strained to listen, silent with dread. By the time he read the ninth name without saying Papa's, I was dizzy from breathing hard. At the tenth, Mama grabbed my hand. Upon hearing the eleventh, Mrs. Campbell whispered, "Please Lord, not my son. Willie is my only child."

At the twelfth name, a woman farther up the line collapsed. Her loud sobs brought others to her side.

The soldier then read the thirteenth name,

the fourteenth, and finally the fifteenth. Mama choked back tears of relief.

Papa was not on the list, nor was Willie.

We know not if they were among the wounded. But at least they are alive.

A long afternoon

Mama and I hiked through the woods with Mrs. Campbell to visit the wounded. We took our canteens. Miss Lulu insisted on staying behind with Johnny and the girls. She does not seem worried about her husband.

We searched the pallets of bandaged and groaning men. Many appeared to be sleeping; some still wore bloody uniforms. Women were tending to the wounds. We kneeled in the dirt, offering sips of water until our canteens were empty. A Negro soldier told us his name is Victor. When we asked if he would like for us to talk to his wife, he said he has no family.

It was a selfish joy that we did not find Papa or Willie there.

. . . .

At night the moon hangs over us like a lantern. It is so bright I lie awake. The river appears to wiggle with light and I can see clouds of mosquitoes over its surface. I think and wonder and worry, now troubled by news from Pluckemin, New Jersey:

Baby Julia Knox died of fever three weeks ago.

July 20, 1779, Tuesday

Another very hot morning. We are moving out so I shall be quick with my pen.

"On to West Point!" came the horseman's cry at sunrise. "Ready yourselves. It's ten miles north."

He shouted today's date, thus I learned it is the twentieth of July. We had been eating plums and pecans gathered yesterday from a farmer's orchard. Right then, Sally and I knew to fill our pockets and get ready. We can finish breakfast while walking, but already there are purple stains on our skirts!

Mama hurried with Johnny to the tiny creek, to wash his bottom — not the large, fast creek where we've been getting our drinking water, but the smaller one. She called over her shoulder to us, smiling: "Perhaps we shall see Papa in a few days."

We are getting faster with packing. In just minutes Sally, Mazie, and I can roll up blankets with our cloaks and shawls, fill our canteens, then gather up spoons and such to carry in our linen bags. We made a sling from ropes so Miss Lulu's tarp will fit over a shoulder. Mrs. Campbell empties our kettle onto the fire to put out the flames. We all take turns at everything.

On the road when Johnny gets too heavy for me, Miss Lulu hefts him into her strong arms. "Come here, lil' one," she says in her husky voice. "Let's give your sister a rest. 'Sides, I ain't had a fine boy like you to hold in a long time."

When Miss Lulu says this, I watch her dark face and her brown eyes, wondering what she means. Has she lost a son like Mama has? Also I wonder why she does not speak of her husband.

West Point, New York

We are camped on a bluff overlooking the Hudson River. A breeze off the water makes it cooler up here. Headquarters is in a Mr. Moore's house, and nearby are rows of tents for soldiers. The Army has issued tents for us ladies as well, and assigned us to a mess. That means we cook for about 30 men, also do laundry and mending.

When soldiers are on the march they do their own cooking, but I am pleased to say that while here at West Point we get to cook for Papa and Willie's brigade. It is a happy circumstance because at long last we are together for breakfast and supper. Our new home has no walls or roof, but is under a wide blue sky. Seagulls serenade us.

Each soldier has his own tin plate and cup, spoon, knife, and fork. After meals they wipe them clean with their sleeves. We have no brick ovens in which to bake loaves of bread, but Miss Lulu's kettle with its firm lid holds enough heat for biscuits to cook nicely.

Mr. Campbell joins us around the fire after his blacksmithing. He makes horseshoes and repairs wagons and harnesses. Yesterday when we gathered for supper, he clamped Willie on the shoulder.

"Miss you, Son. After the war we can get back to working together."

"I look forward to that day, Father." Willie is taller than most of the men. When he sits in the dirt with his plate, his bare knees stick out of his breeches. He is seventeen years old.

"Abby," he said to me, his mouth full of food, "there's something 'specially good about these beans tonight."

"Must be the pot we cooked them in," I answered.

"Oh? How's that?"

I waited for him to take another big bite then said, "It's the same one we washed your shirts in today, Willie." I expected him to gag or spit everything out, but he didn't. He just kept on eating.

"Like I said, Abby, they taste 'specially good."

I felt my cheeks grow hot and was glad it was dark. But in the firelight I could see Mama and Mrs. Campbell exchange a smile.

August 1, 1779, Sunday

A mystery in the woods!

Early this morning Sally, Mazie, and I were gathering sticks and pinecones for our fire. It's a regular routine now. We do this at dawn before the sun gets hot.

While walking under an oak tree, an acorn dropped at our feet, then another.

"Squirrels!" said Sally. "Let's catch one for the skillet."

When an acorn pelted my arm, I stopped. We peered up into the branches.

A boy was looking down at us! He had red hair and was wearing a muddy jacket. His breeches were brown with dirt, his feet bare.

"Hello?" I said.

"Have you some bread?" he asked. His voice was hoarse.

We shook our heads no, still looking up at him.

"Where are your shoes?" Sally asked.

"In the river."

"How old are you?"

"Ten."

"Then what you doin' sittin' in a tree all dirty?" asked Mazie. "Be you hurt?"

The boy laid his head on the wide branch then closed his eyes.

"You can come with us," I said.

When he didn't answer, Mazie nodded. "Uh-*huh*. That be one hungry boy."

Now we are in camp. We did not tell our mothers or Mrs. Campbell about this. If they noticed that we ate only some of our breakfast, they said naught.

Our pockets are full. We shall leave in a moment. I hope he is still there.

Afternoon

We coaxed the boy out of the tree and hid with him in a thicket. He did not want anyone to see him. Then with two hands he shoved the biscuits into his mouth, eating as fast as he could. When he drank from our canteens, water spilled over his chin and down his neck. He was out of breath when he finished.

"Mm," he said. "Now I can go to heaven."

"What happened? Did Indians chase you? We saw one in the woods the other day. Where's your family?" Sally and Mazie peppered him with questions, but I was looking at his jacket of thick wool. The cuffs were torn and most of his buttons were missing. His ankles were covered with scratches and mosquito bites; his feet had purple bruises.

"Who are you hiding from?" I asked.

"The enemy," he replied.

"Well, you are safe with us," Sally told him. "You can stay in our camp. Maybe your mother is with all the other ladies."

"I have no mother." He stood up and took a few steps toward the path, but was limping so badly, he sat down again. I noticed scrapes on his shins, as if he had climbed out of the river onto rocks. "Were you with the soldiers at Stony Point?" I asked.

His green eyes flashed with pride. "Drummer, first class. From the courtyard of King George."

We stared at him. It took a moment for us to understand.

"You're a Redcoat!" Sally cried.

He seemed surprised. "You are loyal to the King, yes?"

"No. Never. We are Patriots!"

Still Sunday—evening by the fire

Thomas Augustus Penny is the boy's name. He fears that General Washington will put him in prison so he refuses to come to our encampment. This morning when we brought him a potato for breakfast he told us he came here from England a few months ago. The ship sailed into New York Harbor and up the Hudson to Stony Point. Some of the British fleet is anchored there now, he said.

"By order of King George the Third, our troops are to tame you rebels. He could have you hanged, did you know that?"

Sally straightened her straw hat then crossed her arms. "We're not afraid of your King. My Papa is a soldier and he's not afraid, either."

"And I'm not afraid of *you*," Thomas said. He bit his lip, then blinked fast. "My father is Major General Penny with the Royal Army. He and his men are looking for me. They shall find me and take me back to our ship. They do not like sassy girls, so I warn you."

Sally and Mazie gave me a questioning look. I knew I must be the one to tell him.

"Thomas," I said as gently as possible, "the Americans captured your father's soldiers at Stony Point. Most of them are in a prison camp now. The ships have sailed away."

Thomas was still blinking. I am only three years older than he, but I wanted to brush the leaves out of his red hair. I wanted to give him a pretty answer.

"Many were wounded," I went on. "Many were killed. We are sorry your father doesn't know where you are."

"Liars!" he cried. He made fists but kept them at his side. "My father is coming for me. I'm waiting for him. Leave me alone!"

We watched him run into the woods.

Now it is time to help with supper. I feel heartsore for Thomas. If we tell Papa, soldiers might go looking, not to hurt or scare him, but to keep him from starving. He is just a boy.

August 2, 1779, Monday

After breakfast Mazie, Sister, and I filled our tin cups with walnuts we had shelled and some cherries. We could not find Thomas. We looked through the forest where we had seen him last, but found only his footprints by the creek.

"Thomas!" we called. "Don't be afraid. Please come to camp." When he didn't appear, we left the food below the oak tree. Sally left her cup for him.

"He needs something that is his very own," she explained.

August 3, 1779, Tuesday

Still at West Point. Every morning at dawn a soldier plays reveille on a cornet. It sounds like a quick, happy march. This wakes the men and lets them know we women are preparing breakfast. A pot of water on the coals takes nearly an hour to boil for coffee but we start before sunrise. After their meal, the soldiers clean weapons and artillery, and drill on the parade grounds. Also, they are building redoubts on two of the hills. These are small, enclosed fortresses that will stand up to enemy cannon fire. Our Continental Army must be ready for battle at any moment.

I ladled coffee into Papa's cup. He said General

Washington watches the river for British ships. The Redcoats are amassing troops in the city of New York, which is less than 50 miles away. And many more are in the southern colonies.

He stirred his biscuit through his plate of gravy, then ate hungrily. After a swallow of coffee he said, "Washington grows more nervous by the hour. Any day now, the French fleet should land in America, with more soldiers and supplies to help us. Lord willing, their ships have not sunk in the Atlantic."

This is the sad truth: If the French don't come soon, we will not be able to stand up to the enemy. We shall lose our independence and suffer under the tyranny of King George.

After visiting the oak tree

The food we left yesterday for Thomas was gone.

Mazie bent low to look for crumbs. "Raccoons or deer could've ate it," she said.

Then Sally cried, "But raccoons and deer don't drink out of cups!" She pointed to the creek. Upside down on a rock, neatly placed, was her tin cup. In the sand beside it someone had scrawled the initials "T. A. P."

"Thomas Augustus Penny," I said aloud, glad to see that he'd been there.

We called and searched, but left without finding him.

August 4, 1779, Wednesday

Baths. This morning Mama insisted we bathe in the creek in our shifts, while we rinse our gowns, aprons, and caps. They are drying in the sun as I write this, and as I keep an eye on Johnny. He is napping beside me in the shady grass. Sally and Mazie are playing tag among the tents with some little boys. Our mothers are mending uniforms under a spreading maple tree.

Oh, the heat is brutal. Even though the necessaries are downwind of camp, a breeze brings the stink and flies. This long, narrow pit is where we — and all the soldiers — sit to ease ourselves. It is not private like a privy with a door, or chamber pot in a house. We girls loathe going there, but we stay together and are quick. Once a week, men fill it up with dirt then dig a new one.

General Washington has ordered cleanliness. If any soldier does not use the necessary but instead eases himself by a tree or in a stream, he shall be fined one dollar. This dollar will be paid to the person who catches him. If women or children are caught, we shall be forced out of camp.

I can hear fifes and drums from the parade ground. These musicians are mostly boys the age of Thomas. I worry about him being in the forest with no food or family.

An idea

During supper last night I spooned out hasty pudding onto the men's plates. They were seated on tree stumps, rocks, and in the dirt. When I came to Willie, I whispered, "Could you please help us tomorrow morning?"

He smiled. "Anything you ask."

August 5, 1779, Thursday

At sunrise Willie walked with us girls to the oak tree. Mrs. Campbell has mended his uniform several times but patches at his knees are unraveling. His legs are bare for want of stockings, and his shoes have come apart at the toes. His tricorn is also battered, but still he looks like a proud Continental soldier.

And tucked into his waist this morning was a slingshot he made last night after supper. It is a branch in the shape of the letter Y with a tight strip of canvas in between.

"See, they're everywhere," Sally reported, picking up acorns and piling them by a rock. We waited in the shade, not speaking.

Soon enough, a squirrel darted by. It picked up an acorn with its tiny front paws, sat on its haunches, and began a noisy gnawing. Before it could finish, Willie launched a stone from his slingshot, knocking the squirrel dead. Soon he had killed two more.

While he skewered the little animals on a stick to carry back to camp, we heard rustling in the brush. As I had hoped, Thomas appeared. He crawled out from the hollow of a fallen tree, covered with pine needles. He looked thin and more tired than before, but his eyes were bright. He said, "Might I have a try at that, sir?"

"Indeed," Willie answered. "But, I am no 'sir.' Willie Campbell is my name. I am still very much a lad like yourself."

Thomas held the slingshot with trembling hands. He took aim but he lacked strength to launch the stone. It landed at his feet.

"May I try again, sir?"

"Here you go, friend. Then afterward, we are going to get some hot food in your belly."

Willie put his strong hands over Thomas's, then together they pulled back the sling. It was a perfect hit. Thrice more and we had seven plump squirrels. They each held one end of the stick as we walked to camp, Thomas limping on his sore feet. His face lit up when he saw our tents and cooking fire, and all the children playing.

His ragged appearance must have touched our mothers' hearts, because without a word they set to caring for him. Miss Lulu plopped him down so she could wash the scrapes on his face and legs.

Mrs. Campbell removed his muddy jacket and replaced it with a clean shirt from her mending bag. I helped Mama skin those squirrels. Then she fried them in sizzling pork fat with mushrooms and onions she had gathered in the forest.

It was the most delicious breakfast since our long journey began. Papa is with us. Thomas is no longer alone in the woods. And every time Willie Campbell is near, I feel happy.

September 17, 1779, Friday

Fall is here. The air is cooler. Leaves on the trees are turning scarlet, gold, and purple, earlier than I remember from last year. Papa said we are farther north than Valley Forge, but even so it could mean that we're in for a hard winter.

"Muskrats and beavers are building their huts with more layers of mud than usual," he told us. "Somehow animals know to prepare."

Before bed last night, Mama was unsnarling Sally's hair with Mrs. Campbell's brush.

"Mama, when will the war end? I want Papa to take us back home."

In the candlelight I could see Mama sigh. There was no use in reminding Sally that we have no home to return to. She hugged my sister but gave no answer.

September 24, 1779, Friday

Still at West Point. Thomas has asked us to call him Tom, which I shall try to do. He sleeps inside our tent by the doorway. He has no blanket, so I gave him mine. My cloak is warm enough when I wrap it around me and tuck my knees to my chest.

This morning he helped Sally and me carry water from the stream up to the laundry kettle. He is talkative now that he's not so hungry. He told us what happened at Stony Point.

"I was asleep," he said. "It was the middle of the night. I could not find my father in the noise and smoke so I ran to the river where our ships were anchored. Men were starting to row a boat away from shore. I tried to climb aboard but it was so dark, an oar knocked me on the head. I fell in the water. It was cold and the wind made waves."

"And you lost your shoes," Sally said.

"Yes." Thomas lifted the pot he was carrying and poured it into the large kettle.

"I lost my shoes, too," said my sister in her way of showing sympathy. "Last winter in the mud. My feet were dreadful cold. Maybe our Army will give you a pair."

Just then a captain approached us. "Thomas A. Penny?" he asked.

"Yes, sir."

"You may stay with the Continental Army, but you must work. Since we need a drummer, what say you to that?"

"Thank you, sir," Tom replied. "But King George could have my head for being a traitor. And my father would be angry with me if I play music for the American soldiers. Tomorrow I am leaving to search for him."

"Laddie." The captain removed his tricorn and held it at his side. "We have no British officer by the name you gave us, Augustus Thomas Penny, among the wounded or captured. Your father is missing. Either he ran away from his command

and is hiding somewhere, or he drowned in the Hudson. Many did, you know, but we shall never learn their names. Their bodies have drifted out to sea by now. I'm sorry to give it to you like this, lad."

"My father would never run or hide! He is honourable." Thomas's chin quivered.

I held back my tears. It seems there were no pretty words for Thomas today.

By candle, in our tent

Willie touched my elbow tonight after supper. When I turned to look up at him, he slipped a folded piece of paper into my hand then closed his around mine.

"Read this," he instructed. "Then burn it."

"What is it?"

"I found it nailed to the wall in the supply room. I searched all over, in every building and Headquarters, but thank goodness it's the only copy." Then he left, walking in the darkness to his tent.

I have just dropped the paper into the fire. Not until it flamed and burned to ash did I come into this tent for my diary.

Willie had given me an advertisement about a runaway slave named Tilda and her eight-year-old daughter, Philomena. Tilda is passing herself as a free woman and pretends that she has a husband in the Continental Army. Their master wants them back. Reward for their return is 50 dollars.

The description matched Miss Lulu and Mazie.

September 27, 1779, Monday

Still at West Point. We are waiting with the soldiers for orders to march. I pray we get to the winter camp before it snows. Last night I could not sleep. The ground was cold beneath me and I kept thinking about our friends. If they are runaway slaves, I do not blame them, nor does Willie.

Must I keep this news to myself?

September 30, 1779, Thursday

West Point. Rations are low. Daily, each soldier gets one pound of beef or pork and one pound of flour. The Army gives women half, sometimes three-quarters, and their children a quarter. Today I smelled rot in our pork and saw tiny white dots. Maggots. To cover the bad taste we add as much pepper as our tongues will bear.

The men are cheered when we can give them hot coffee with each meal. We grind the beans between two stones then add shredded hickory bark to make it taste stronger. Often dirt ends up in the bottom of their cups.

"'Tis the best we can do," an orderly told us. "The French ships are full of food and new uniforms, but they are nowhere in sight. General Washington is deeply concerned."

He told us about another concern: Indians who have been helping the Redcoats. General Washington said that before there would be any peace talks with the tribes, he was going to teach them a lesson. In the spring he ordered two generals, Sullivan and Clinton, to destroy the Iroquois settlements in western New York.

This morning an express rider brought news to camp. "The Sullivan-Clinton campaign just ended," he shouted. "'Twas a complete victory. It took months, but the Iroquois Confederacy shall trouble us no longer."

From the saddle of his horse, he described the events. Thousands of our soldiers burned all the grain and vegetable crops, the cornfields, and fruit orchards. They set torches to the longhouses. Forty villages went up in flames. Now there will be no fall harvest and nothing for the Indians to plant in the spring. Many warriors died defending their homes, many were captured, then marched to a prison camp.

My mother yelled a question, same as she had about the British ship that sank. "Sir, what about the women and children? Winter is coming. Where shall the families live?"

"Madam, I do not know. Nor do I care. They were aiding the enemy."

Mama looked at me with sad eyes. "Oh Abby, at least when our house burned it was only because of the wind."

October 2, 1779, Saturday

Miss Lulu baked a honey cake for supper. It wasn't really a cake and there was no honey.

"I jess call it that to make it seem better," she said while passing around slices of unsalted flatbread. "Sometimes thas all y'can do, is pretend."

Willie and I exchanged glances in the firelight. We had not spoken of the runaway slaves, but he did tell me if he found any more handbills about Tilda and her daughter, he would rip them down. "There are Negroes in our ranks here," he said. "Not a lot, but some freed slaves who've been promised their own land when the war is over. Far as I know, no one has bothered to ask if they have wives here. Abby, let's just hope no officer comes around and asks Miss Lulu to point out her husband."

At night before I sleep I pray for our new friends Mazie, Miss Lulu, and Thomas. Now I've added another prayer: Lord, please watch over Willie Campbell. He is honourable and kind. I like him. Thank You. Amen.

November 9, 1779, Tuesday

Still at West Point. For some weeks I have not written for want of ink. At least quills are easier to find. Though I prefer a goose or swan feather, crows often drop one of theirs while squabbling high in a tree. When it floats to the ground, I have a new pen. I need only to use Mama's knife to shape the nib.

This morning Willie slipped something into my hand. It crackled like paper. My heart raced, fearing it was another notice about the runaway slaves, Tilda and Philomena. Indeed, it was paper, but folded inside was ink powder. He got it from the quartermaster in charge of supplies. There were no new shirts or stockings or wool cloaks, but there was a small tin of ink.

Thus, I return to my quiet friend, this diary. I adore Willie for thinking of me, and hope I can do something kind for him.

Every day is colder. Skies are gray. A comfort is the fire. We turn ourselves like a roasting duck, facing the flames for a few moments, then turning to warm our backs. Often there is the smell of singed leather from those sitting with outstretched legs, trying to warm feet. In our tent, we have laid down boughs of pine so that we are not sleeping on the frozen ground. Oh, they make a prickly mattress!

Thomas was given a drum and sticks. Then he was issued a ragged blanket, breeches, and a blue jacket taken from a soldier who died of dysentery. His new shoes have holes where his toes poke out, but he stands as proud as if his uniform is new. He has joined the other boys who play music while the men drill.

"My father would not have wanted me to die alone in the woods," he told us, about his decision to stay. "I like you rebels. When my mother was alive, she said the American colonies are full of brave people. I think she would be glad to know I'm here."

Sally tells everyone, "Tom Penny is my new brother." And *he* tells everyone, "Sally Stewart is a pest," but he then gives a playful tug to the strings of her cap.

A cold afternoon

Food rations are less each day. Dry wood for the campfires is harder to find. And ammunition is so scarce that the soldiers have stopped firing the morning and evening guns.

General Washington is worried about his young friend the Marquis de Lafayette. "The French should have come by now," he tells his officers who tell their men, like Papa and Willie. "A hurricane may have sunk the ships."

I remember Lafayette from Valley Forge. He dined with some of the American officers when he visited Headquarters. Sally and I had giggled to see him holding his teacup with his little finger in the air. He is a polite Frenchman, twenty-two years of age. He sailed back to France to get help for the Americans, but it's been nearly a year. That is why the general is so worried.

News from the South is grim. The British are in complete control of Georgia.

November 17, 1779, Wednesday

Last night we awoke to a woman screaming. When Sally, Mazie, and I realized our mothers were not in our tent we were frightened. But soon someone came with a lantern and peeked in on us. It was Mrs. Campbell.

"All is well," she replied to our questions. "Emma Smith has delivered a fine little girl. Her name is Liberty."

We could hear what sounded like a kitten mewing in the distance, but it was the newborn baby.

Drifting back to sleep I thought of Elisabeth. I miss her. She would love our new friend, Thomas. She would share my worry that Miss Lulu and Mazie might be runaways and be caught. We would whisper about Willie Campbell and her Ben Valentine. But I'm happy that when her child is born she will be in a house, not in a cold tent with little food to eat.

End of November 1779

Last day at West Point. Snow is falling.

We leave tomorrow at dawn for the winter

encampment in Morristown, New Jersey. I am uneasy about the march before us — heading south three or four days through the frozen woods. Everyone will go. First the soldiers and officers, horses pulling cannons on two-wheeled carriages, then blacksmiths, cobblers, and supply wagons carrying all the tents, including ours.

Women and children shall bring up the rear.

General Sullivan and other generals, who have been at different posts in these colonies, will also march their units to Morristown.

Mrs. Campbell is very kind to us. She had enough woolen yarn to knit six mittens, so we three girls each have one and our mothers each have one. It is better than none at all. I can keep one hand warm in a pocket while the mittened one is out. They are gray and itchy but bring much comfort.

I like being near her. Because she is Willie's mother, somehow I feel closer to him.

Johnny has grown in the four months that we have been at West Point. He is big enough to walk on his own now. We have told him he must hold on to Mama's skirt or mine, so that we know he is still with us. Because of the small children and wagons, our train will be slow—at least two days behind the soldiers.

December 3, 1779, Friday

Morristown, New Jersey. It is afternoon. I write this from our tent as wind shakes the sides and ruffles the pages of this diary. Sally and Johnny, all of us are still cold from our three-day journey.

We arrived yesterday in a blizzard, trudging through snow up to my knees. The encampment is in a hollow—Jockey Hollow—surrounded by a dense forest, frosted white. The Wick family owns this land and is sharing their farmhouse with General St. Clair.

Finally the men have their tents. Until our supply wagons rolled in, they were forced to sleep in the open with only the trees for protection. I cannot imagine how they must have suffered in this bitter cold, my poor Papa and Willie, too. Though snow is now swirling in a vicious wind, we can hear the ring of hatchets in the woods. Soldiers are building log huts, hundreds and hundreds of them, for much of the entire Continental Army shall be gathered here in the coming days.

I'm ashamed of myself for complaining, but it was *misery* setting up our tent in the storm, trying to hammer stakes into the ground as the wind kept sweeping the canvas out of our hands. Finally the eight of us were able to take shelter: Mama, Sally, Johnny, and I; Miss Lulu and Mazie; and Mrs. Campbell and Tom Penny, whom she has taken under her wing.

"Tomorrow will be better," Mother has assured us. I think she means that at least we are no longer following wagons on a frozen road.

Headquarters is a few miles from Jockey Hollow, in a mansion owned by a war widow, Mrs. Theodosia Ford. She has several children, including her son Jacob, already a soldier but still in his teens.

Martha Washington is traveling here from Mount Vernon, to spend the winter. She will be here for Christmas. Am I selfish to want to visit her again in a warm kitchen? The memory of her spicy gingerbread makes my stomach tighten with hunger.

Just an hour ago Papa and Willie found us here in our tent. I was happy to see my father, but more so Willie. They stepped inside to make sure we had arrived safely and that Johnny hadn't gotten lost or frozen his little toes. Wind howled and battered our canvas walls as we encouraged one another.

"Thirteen thousand men shall soon be here," Papa said, "coming from all over. Rations are low and so far this is a cruel winter, but our families will do fine, I am certain of it." He nodded to Miss Lulu and Mrs. Campbell, by way of including them.

He hugged Mother and us girls, then he hugged Mazie, who smiled up at him. As they left, Willie's hand brushed mine. His touch made me feel hopeful. For what, I am not sure.

Second week of December 1779

Still snowing. We woke this morning to silence. The wind had stopped. I peeked out to see that we are buried in drifts of snow. All around us, mounds of white are jiggling as women push their way out of their tents to start their cooking fires.

We save our coals in an iron pot and keep them with us through the long night. For kindling we unravel what's left of our sun hats, feeding in bits of straw, and blowing until they catch aflame. Then we carry the pot outside. Even using a mitten, my hands and arms are numb by the time we clear away the fresh snow for our fire.

I do not know what day it is. Sometimes my ink doesn't thaw until evening but by then my eyes are heavy and the cold draws us into our blankets. All eight of us huddle together like a family of squirrels in a nest.

Mercury, 8 degrees

At noon today, Thomas and I carried a kettle of soup to the Pennsylvania Brigade, along a path stomped down by the soldiers. It was as if we were passing through a tunnel, for the snow on either side was up to our shoulders.

Truth is, the only reason I was cheerful on this errand was my hope to see Willie. When I ladled soup into his bowl I gave him an extra spoonful from my portion. He held the bowl with his red, chapped hands. "Thank you, Abby. It does me good to see you today."

Dozens of huts are almost finished. Most have walls of logs five feet high and are getting taller as the men keep cutting trees and dragging them from the woods. Soon the forest will be bare. Mr. Campbell works with a group who notch the ends of the logs so they will fit together at the corners. Then they fill spaces with clay down the length of the logs, to keep the wind from blowing inside.

Twelve soldiers will sleep in each tiny hut, most of them sitting up for want of beds.

"By Christmas, we hope to have everyone under a roof," Papa told us. "That means women and children, too." His breath was a frozen cloud between us. My father is chilled in his thin jacket and wet shoes, I can tell. All the men are cold. They shiver violently if they stop for a moment to rest, so they keep working.

We eat once a day. We, and especially the men working so hard, cannot begin to warm our insides without drinking a cup of hot water.

There is no more coffee or tea or flour. No vegetables or fruit. Beef is half rations.

Yesterday a villager drove through camp in his sleigh, throwing a chunk of meat to each campfire. It was fresh, and left blood in the snow. Shouts of "Bless you, sir!" filled the cold air.

Miss Lulu sniffed it before dropping it into our pot. "Poor ole horse," she said. "I jess wish we had some onions and yams to make the men a nice stew. They gonna blow away in the wind if they don't eat more."

December 13, 1779, Monday

Snowing again, Jockey Hollow. When we're outside by our fire, we hear news from soldiers walking among the tents and nearly finished huts. These soldiers get *their* news from Headquarters where General Washington hears it from the dispatch riders. But this week, because roads are buried to the fence tops, the messengers came on snowshoes. They hiked for miles and miles, staying overnight with farmers along the way.

It is dangerous to travel. Lady Washington left Virginia a month ago, heading north in a coach, but blizzards have stranded her in Philadelphia. She will not be here by Christmas after all.

We are hungry all the time, and cold. Sally and I take turns sharing our soup with Johnny, then Mazie shares with him. He is listless and pale. This morning when we unwrapped the rags from his feet to put on dry ones, we noticed black spots on his toes.

"Oh, Lord," said Mama in a hush.

Last winter when the Army was in Valley Forge, I saw soldiers with feet blackened from frostbite. The surgeons amputated. That is how Helen Kern's husband died and why she came to live with us.

We are in a quiet panic to keep my brother warm.

Christmas Eve, 1779, Friday

I am writing without a candle tonight. The walls of our tent are aglow from a full moon. There are just seven of us now, for Thomas has insisted on helping Papa and Willie work on the log huts and stay with them. He is ragged in his uniform and torn shoes, but already Tom is a proud American soldier.

It seems as if we have a smoky fire in here, but it is just the frost from our breathing. We are trying to get warm by holding our cups of hot water to our chests, and sipping bit by bit.

Johnny has a fever.

Christmas Day, 1779, Saturday

Snowing again.

Explosions awoke us this morning. I was too cold to be afraid. What I mean is that if the British were firing cannons at us, it would be death if we fled in the snow. There is nowhere to hide without freezing.

A soldier told us the men are merely blowing up tree stumps with gunpowder. The ground is too frozen to dig them out and they need to chop them for firewood.

Many of the huts are finished. Jockey Hollow looks like a city of log cabins, all in neat rows. I heard someone calling my name. Willie was waving me over to one of the huts with most of its roof on.

"This small one here is for you ladies, behind ours. Inside, I hammered pegs near both sides of the hearth, so you can hang your cloaks to dry. We shall be neighbours, Abby. There are more being built for the other women, see?" He pointed down a row.

I stepped through the opening where a door was to be hung. A fireplace was at the opposite wall. I touched a log beam overhead, looking up though a gap, snowflakes landing on my face. Willie must have seen my smile.

"Like a Queen's castle, yes?"

"Oh yes, Willie, a castle. We shall finally get warm here."

Papa and Mr. Campbell appeared, carrying planks of wood to layer over the roof. "Not too soon, either," Papa said. "The rivers are freezing so the sawmills can no longer run. The waterwheels get stuck in the ice. Daughter, let your mother and the others know. This shall be a merry Christmas after all!"

"Yes, Papa!"

I did not tell him Johnny is sick.

December 28, 1779, Tuesday

Soldiers have spread hay over the snow, among the cabins—it is drier walking around—but it has brought a reprimand from General Washington. Just as I was returning to our tent, the General rode through camp. He looks gallant in the saddle, his heavy wool cape draped over his horse's flank, his tricorn firm on his head.

"What in heaven's name!" he yelled to one of his officers. "Our animals will starve if you trample their fodder like this. And the same goes for gunpowder. How will we stand up to the enemy with such waste? No more of this, understand?"

The officer saluted. "Sir! Yes sir, Your Excellency!"

We are in our new home. Oh joy, four walls, a roof, and a warm fire. The floor is dirt, but we have laid down pine boughs from the cut trees. After serving soup to the men, we gathered in our hut with Papa, Willie, and Tom Penny.

"Merry Christmas!" we said to one another. Our drink of cheer was hot water. Sally and Mazie led us in a clapping song they've been practicing. But when Papa noticed that Johnny wasn't laughing and that his cheeks were scarlet with fever, he took him from Mama. He held him tight against his shoulder.

"Johnny, brave boy," he said. "We shall need your strong arms when the war is over, to build our house." I heard a catch in my father's voice. "Rally now, my son. It's Christmas."

Tom came over and patted Johnny's head. "There's a good laddie. When you feel better, you may bang on my drum all you want."

Then it was time to say good night.

"Merry Christmas, Abigail!" Willie called, turning to wave. He walked with Papa and Thomas through the snow, the sky bright with the rising moon.

Moments later, wind announced another storm. An icy draft comes under our door. We have stuffed the gap with canvas, but still the coals in our fire flare with a breeze.

Now to sleep.

January 3, 1780, Monday

Johnny is still fevered. We do not know what to do but rub warmth into his toes and feed him broth. When he tries to walk, he whimpers. If he wants to move around the hut, he crawls. I die inside worrying that a surgeon might cut off the feet of our little baby.

"Abby, dear," said Mama, "when the skies clear, will you please go for help? I hear there's a doctor near Headquarters and Lady Washington should be there by now. Perhaps there is some medicine—"

"I'll go, Mother."

While we wait in this storm, I try to teach the younger children. It has been nearly a year since we last attended school! I invited Thomas. He thought a moment then said, "Thank you, Abby, but I like working with the men, also playing my drum when they march. They need me."

My students are Mazie, Sally, Robert, who also is eight, and his sister, Anna, who is eleven. She brought her own quill and ink jug as she, too, keeps a diary! Robert and Anna are Mrs. Ewing's children, in the hut next to ours.

We have no books or newspapers, so I tore some empty pages from this journal and printed words for them in big letters. I made up a story for the younger ones to read, and Anna wrote her own. They are fast learners!

Then they took turns with the pens, first writing numbers then writing their names. While Mazie spelled out hers, she squinted in concentration, whispering to herself. Too soon I realized she was writing "P-H-I-L-O-M-E-N-A." Quickly I ran my finger over the letters to smear the ink and shook my head no at her. She looked up, startled, as fear came into her eyes. It seemed that for a moment she had forgotten to pretend.

"Like this, Mazie," I said, carefully printing "M-A-Z-I-E." "Write it three times to help you remember."

I glanced over at Miss Lulu, who was by the fire warming Johnny's feet in her hands. She had been watching us. She gave me a slight nod, as if we now shared something.

Later

In this small cabin there is no place to hide my diary so when I am up and about I keep it in my right pocket, my ink and quill in my left pocket. Now that I know Sally can read very well, and so can Mazie, I fear their curiosity. They stare when I am writing, such as now! Am kneeling by the fire for light, my back turned to them.

"What say you, Abby?" my sister asks, trying to peek over my shoulder.

Mazie answers for me, "Uh-*huh*. A little this and a little that."

It has been one year since our house in Valley Forge burned to the ground. One year since I've seen my friends. Do they wonder about me? At night I think of them as I drift to sleep in prayer: Lucy, Molly, Naomi, Ruth. . . .

January 8, 1780, Saturday

Morristown Headquarters, in Mrs. Ford's mansion. Odd circumstances have placed me in this crowded house, now for the past two days. The view out these windows is solid white.

The blizzard before this one stopped long enough for me to gather my cloak and wrap rags around my feet. Sally gave me her mitten so I would have one for each hand. Then out of the hut I ran, slipping along the hilly path to Headquarters.

After some minutes, I heard, "Abby! Wait!"

I turned to see Mazie waving.

"Go back!" I yelled.

"Please, Abby, I want to see the General's lady. You said she be kind and good."

I looked at the sky growing dark again. If Mazie returned as the storm hit, she could get lost. She would die without shelter.

"Come, then," I said. "But we must hurry." Already wind was pulling at my cloak and stinging my cheeks. We ran. By the time I pounded on the door of Headquarters, we were shivering. Oney showed us to a blazing hearth and gave us each a cup of hot cider.

"Abby, chile," she scolded. "Does your Mama know where you are?"

"Yes, Oney."

Hand on her wide hip she glared at Mazie. "You, chile?"

Mazie looked down at her wet shoes. "Mammy thinks I be at the necessary."

Oh dear, I thought. Miss Lulu must fear Mazie has perished and Mama will wonder the same about me. Two mothers are worrying.

By Mrs. Ford's grate

Everyone who happened to be under this roof when the storm struck is now stranded with Mrs. Ford and her children. General Washington is here with his servants, staff, and aides-de-camp, also officers who had been meeting with him, several soldiers, and guards. The guard huts are just across the way, but the drifts from here to there are so deep—coming up to the men's shoulders—that they cannot start digging until there is a lull in the wind.

There are so many people here that everyone

bumps into one another going from room to room — through the halls, and up and down the narrow staircase. If two meet on the steps, one must turn sideways to let the other pass.

I can hear coughing and sneezing all through this house. Lady Washington is in her room upstairs. After her long trip by sleigh she took a chill and now has a cold.

No doctor is here, nor any medicine for Johnny. And something else has upset me: This morning a captain gave Mazie a hard look.

"Girl, where are you from?"

"A long ways away, sir," she answered.

"What's your name? And what is your mother's name?"

His questions made me nervous. It seemed he knew about the runaway slaves Tilda and Philomena.

Mazie lifted her chin. "Sir, I be Mazie. Miss Lulu be my mammy."

"I see. And what brigade might your father be in?"

"Dunno, sir."

"Then what is his name?"

"I call him Pappy."

The captain opened his mouth for a loud sneeze. He wiped his nose with his hand then dried his hand on his vest. "Well then, little girl, when this wind stops we shall go find your *pappy*. I'm certain you shall be glad to introduce us."

Oh, for this storm to end! I'm worried about Johnny, and I'm desperate to warn Miss Lulu. For pretending to have a soldier husband, she and Mazie could be cast out of the Army in this cruel winter. Or be put in prison until their master comes for them.

Later, still January 8

It is shameful for me to eavesdrop, but I like to hear news.

While in a crowded hallway, I heard soldiers complain about Benedict Arnold. He was court-martialed just before Christmas, in a trial at Norris's Tavern. That is just up the road from here. Several officers accused him of being dishonest and greedy while he was in charge of Philadelphia. He used government wagons for his personal pleasure, so was sentenced to a reprimand. This means a public scolding by General Washington.

I also heard officers fretting about the Marquis de Lafayette and the French Navy. There has been a terrible shipwreck on one of our shores.

January 9, 1780, Sunday

Still at the Ford Mansion. Sun is shining and the wind has stopped! The mercury reads 20 degrees. In a few minutes we shall finally be able to leave Headquarters.

Hundreds of men from the surrounding farms and villages have come with sleds, horses, and wagons. They are working in teams, and with our soldiers, to clear the roads so that supplies can reach Jockey Hollow.

Such good news, but all I can think is that Mazie and I must hurry, hurry home!

January 10, 1780, Monday

Home again, in our hut. Miss Lulu near collapsed with relief when Mazie and I came through the door. As Mama hugged me, my eyes searched the small room. I did not see my brother.

"Johnny?" My voice was hoarse. I have a cold now as well.

Mama pointed to a mound of blankets in the corner. My heart stopped for a moment, truly it did.

Before I could cry out, the blanket moved. My brother's face smiled up at me. He had been playing hide-and-seek with Sally.

"Johnny boy!" I cried, swooping him up into my arms.

"Last night his fever left," Mama said. "Keeping his little feet warm was the best thing we did, Abby."

I told Miss Lulu what happened at Headquarters.

Her brown eyes looked sad. "I 'spect you folks know me and Mazie got no man here. My husband drowned in a river when we was on the run, been some months now."

"Where did you come from?" Sally blurted before we could offer our condolences.

"From a place we ain't never going back to."

January 12, 1780, Wednesday

Now that some of the roads have been cleared, farmers are driving sleds of hay and provisions into Jockey Hollow, as well as cattle for slaughter. These kind neighbours are trusting the Army to pay them, but there is no money, not even for soldiers' wages. Many are deserting.

"Our Continental dollar is a worthless piece of paper," Papa told us this morning when we brought a pail of hot coffee. The men held out their cups, thanking us as we went around with our ladle.

Papa explained, "Almost daily, a starving fellow walks out of this camp, headed for home where he shall have the comfort of bed and bread. That is, if he doesn't freeze to death on the way."

An odd sight this afternoon: As the cattle were coming *into* pens at the edge of camp, horses were going *out*. General Washington is sending the draft animals to different farms about the countryside, where feed is available.

It is a gamble. If they stay here, they will starve and die, but if the British attack, we are doomed.

General Knox would need his artillery horses to pull the cannons, to form a line of defense. Cows would be no help at all. They are slow and do not obey orders.

January 18, 1780, Tuesday

My cold is somewhat better. At noon I stepped outside to ease myself. The captain who had questioned Mazie was walking among the women's huts. My heart dropped. I hurried inside.

"Miss Lulu," I cried. "He's coming, that man we told you about. What if he makes you leave camp?"

She was holding Johnny on her hip. She put him down by the fire with Sally, then patted my shoulder. "Things gonna be jess fine, Abigail."

A light snow was falling when the captain came to our door. While he questioned Miss Lulu, I scarce could breathe. Mama and Mrs. Campbell were quiet.

"Madam," he said to her. "The name of your husband."

"I call him Han'some. He don't like his real name."

"And what would that be?"

"You got to ask him yourself."

The officer narrowed his eyes. "Then come with me."

Miss Lulu buttoned her cloak and took Mazie's hand. I followed them to the Pennsylvania Brigade where the men were now building officers' quarters. I saw Willie and Thomas hauling a tree from the woods; Papa and Mr. Campbell were chopping branches off another. The forest that had been so dense is becoming a field of stumps.

The captain went up to a Negro hefting a log onto a roof.

"Morning, sir," the man said, saluting the officer when his hands were free.

I recognized him from the wounded at Stony Point. We had given him water. He told us his name was Victor and that he was without a family. Now here he was, meeting Miss Lulu for the first time.

I was afraid for my friends.

Falling snow was clinging to our clothes and covering our trail of footprints. Wind had begun stirring in the few trees that remained. The captain fumed. "I do not have all day, people. Another storm is coming. I ask you, what is your relation?"

At this, Victor's dark face broke into a slow smile. He did not answer the officer, but said, "Mazie, honey, I hoped you was bringin' some of Mammy's good biscuits but your hands are empty, I see."

"We got no flour yet, Pappy."

Miss Lulu walked over to Victor. She was only as tall as his shoulder. She looked up at him with curiosity. Then she touched the sleeve of his coat where his elbow showed through. "I sew'd this last week, Han'some. Now I gots to do it all over again."

"You're a good woman, Miz Lulu."

"I know that." Her cheeks creased with a smile.

I was without words! How had Victor learned their names? And how did he know this captain was going to question him?

Evening, still Tuesday

We are close to the fire, trying to stay warm. We do not have a clock. It feels late because it has been dark for hours. As I write these words, the younger ones are asleep and I am eavesdropping on the lady talk!

It seems that some days ago Mama and Mrs. Campbell searched for Victor. They knew he did not have a wife. They were cautious when telling him about Tilda and her daughter, Philomena. But when they saw his gentleness and that he became concerned for our friends, Mama asked for his help. The good man agreed. All was arranged.

Now the fire is low, the lady talk has become whispers. In the dim light, I can see their tired faces. All evening they have been knitting scarves for the soldiers, from strips of rags. Mama is slow because of her swollen fingers, but she keeps at it. Suddenly she smiled.

"Lulu," she said, "now that you have met Victor, what think you?"

Miss Lulu took her time answering. She watched a log crumble into the coals then poked it with her knitting needle to rouse a flame. "Well," she said, "what I think is this: Soon as this storm lets up, I'm gonna start taking that han'some man his coffee."

February 4, 1780, Friday

I am only thirteen, but this is the cruelest weather of my whole life. There is one storm after another. The huts are nearly buried in snow. The cold makes me want to stay in all day. But this morning when a messenger came with news, we went outside to listen.

He stood on a tree stump so he could be heard, his breath making a cloud of frost. "'Tis the worst winter in a century," he said. "New York Harbor is frozen solid. The Redcoats can walk from island to island on ice eight feet thick. Last week the moon was bright enough for them to march across the Hudson over to New Jersey. They captured two of our fine towns, Newark and Elizabeth."

The messenger then talked about the Indians from last summer. There was no emotion in his voice. "Those Iroquois shall bother us no longer.

Many who fled to Fort Niagara have starved and frozen to death."

I thought of the children. Did they have blackened feet like Johnny, but were unable to get warm? When I imagine their suffering, my heart hurts.

Shelves in the commissary are now empty. All the supplies that the villagers brought were used up within days. The few cows left shall not begin to feed thousands of soldiers. Papa is nervous.

"The men are talking mutiny," he told us. "No food. No warm clothes. No wages for us to purchase any of these things from the village. How does Congress expect our Army to be strong?"

My mother pleaded with him. "Do not let them, Edward, please. Mutineers are hanged or shot, you know that."

Papa went on. "Dear woman, there are two enemies that will destroy our Army: winter and starvation. We must do something."

February 14, 1780, Monday

Blue sky! This morning Sally and I hiked to Headquarters while the sun was shining. The cold was fierce. To keep warm, we swung our arms and walked as fast as we could without slipping. Our purpose was to deliver a note from Mama to Lady Washington.

Mama let Sally dribble wax from our candle onto the letter, to seal it.

Oney led us upstairs to a parlour. It was much the same as Headquarters in Valley Forge, crowded with officers' wives chatting and knitting socks for soldiers. The elegance and the colors of their dresses were beautiful to see. Suddenly I was aware of my unkempt appearance and Sally's. Our sleeves and aprons are no longer white, but are gray and stained. Rags hold our shoes together. We have not bathed in months.

How I hated the war right then and wanted a pretty gown! Embarrassed, I stayed in the hallway but Lady Washington had already noticed us.

"Abby, Sally, how nice to see you girls. Come, please." When she waved us into the room I noticed her dress was different than the other ladies'. It was plain and brown, no lace or layers of petticoats. Her mobcap framed her face without any frills. In an odd way, her simple attire made me feel a bit better about my own.

We gave her Mama's letter. She broke the seal then leaned toward the light of the window to read. I do not know what Mama wrote.

"Lady Washington, are you staying here all winter?" Sally asked. "The cold is most dreadful. You could lose your feet, ma'am!"

Mrs. Washington laughed. "Yes dear, 'tis cold indeed. Even my son, Jacky, urges me to return to Mount Vernon, where 'tis somewhat warmer and my grandchildren miss me. But 'tis the fifth year of this war and the Old Man needs me at his side more than ever. Now girls, please hurry back to your mother lest another storm catch you. I apologize, but we have no sweets for you today."

When Sally and I curtsied good-bye, I noticed that our ragged hems no longer touch the floor. We have grown taller over these long months!

After supper, still Monday

I am thinking about this morning at Head-quarters. Sally and I took our time going down the stairs for there were angry voices. We wanted to listen. Villagers were lined up in the hallways, waiting to see General Washington.

"Your men stole the honey from my beehive. I want payment now!"

"Our fence is missing. Find your own firewood."

"We saw soldiers running from the barn with our shovels and axes."

"Our chickens and hogs are gone."

Sally and I hurried out the front door, holding hands as we ran home. Without speaking, we knew what was happening. Same as in Valley Forge. The Army is looting the countryside.

March 15, 1780, Wednesday

Before bed. For the briefest of moments tonight, we stood outside in the frozen darkness to watch the sky. Colors were rolling across the heavens in waves of purple, green, and red, reflecting off the snow. Somehow I felt comforted by this magical sight.

"'Tis the aurora borealis," explained Mrs. Campbell, who held Johnny warm inside her cloak.

"I like it!" He pointed. "See? See?"

Miss Lulu replied, "Yes, lil' Johnny, we see. Looks like angels be dancing. Beautiful angels."

April 17, 1780, Monday

This morning a soldier in a trim blue coat came to our door. I feared he was coming to take away Miss Lulu, or that he had bad news about Papa.

"I'm looking for Mrs. Stewart," he said, removing his tricorn.

"Yes?" Mama answered. "Is everything all right?" Her voice was shaky. We crowded around her.

He handed her a canvas sack. "Ma'am, this is from Lady Washington, for your daughters. She sends her fond regards, and invites you to tea on the morrow, if there be no storm. Three o'clock."

"Sir," Mama said. "I thank thee." We stared out the door as the soldier returned to the snowy path. Then she opened the sack.

"My word." She pulled out two pairs of ladies' shoes in soft brown leather. There were worn spots on the soles, but they were in good shape.

Sally shrieked with surprise. "Mazie, you and I can share this smaller pair. Oh Mother, thank you!"

"What do you mean, Daughter?"

"Your note to Mrs. Washington. Did you ask her for shoes for us?"

"Sally Stewart, I did no such thing." Mama gave us a serious look. "Did you girls complain about the rags on your feet?"

"No!" my sister and I cried at once.

"Mother, we would *never* do that," I assured her. "There are children in camp who need clothes. Maybe Lady Washington is helping them as well."

"And inviting their mothers to tea?" asked Mrs. Campbell.

We were quiet.

Finally I said, "Mama, what did you write to Mrs. Washington?"

She smoothed her threadbare apron over her skirt, then looked at her hands. They were red and chapped. "I cannot go to tea like this. I have not a proper thing to wear. I need a bath and a brush. Abigail dear, in my letter I reminded Lady Washington that I am praying for her and the General, and praying for all the Army. That is all. I did not ask for shoes."

April 18, 1780, Tuesday

Snow and wind have been battering our hut all day. Mama shall not be going to tea at Headquarters.

Mazie and Sally have invented a dance to entertain us. First they sing and wave their arms then they twirl in their skirts. The finale is a little kick while pointing their toes. We all clapped at the sight of their new shoes, which are quite stylish with a small heel and buckle.

I often think about the elegant ball in Philadelphia. All the ladies danced in shoes like these, barely seen from under the swirl of their gowns.

I was most happy to give my pair to Mazie.

April 26, 1780, Wednesday

I am sitting on a stump on the sunny side of our hut. The air is still cold, but the drifts are melting a bit each day, and at long last the creeks have come alive. We are thrilled to drink water without having to first melt snow.

Finally winter is over. I lost count of the blizzards. Someone said 26. Soldiers who froze to death are few, though some died of pneumonia and infection from frostbite. Once again I thank God for sparing my little brother.

Johnny is full of mischief. For the past week I have been without a quill because he played with mine. He pretended it was a sword and swished it against the walls until the stem broke.

But at this moment, I am able to write because of Willie. This morning after breakfast he surprised me with a cedar writing box. Inside were two goose quills, several packets of ink powder, and a sheaf of paper.

"Where did you get these?" I asked. "The commissary has been empty."

"I did not steal, Abby, I swear to you. One of our messmates did. The fellow would not say where he got these things, so I bought it all from him."

"Then you and Papa have finally received your wages?"

"No. I made a trade. Gave him my hat."

"But your head will be cold, Willie."

He smiled at me then nodded to our row of huts where icicles are melting. "Spring is almost here, Abby. I shall get another hat."

I am touched by Willie's gift. Now I shall try to find him a new tricorn. Sometimes we see them in the road or woods, where soldiers have dropped them.

April 28, 1780, Friday

Birthdays. Sally and Mazie turned nine last month, and I am now fourteen.

Yesterday, a girl in camp named Esther married one of the soldiers. It was a quick wedding with no cake or cider, but they both looked happy. Then she returned to her chores of laundry, which I was doing as well. As she and I hung blankets to dry, I asked her age.

"Fourteen," she replied. Esther then told me

that until the war is over she shall live with her mother, and her husband shall stay with his brigade.

This makes me think of my newlywed sister. We have received no letter from Elisabeth, so we do not know if she has safely delivered her baby.

On the subject of babies, Liberty—who was born before we left West Point—is now five months old. We saw her Mama carrying her through camp in a sling across her chest. Then last night, a lady in a hut near ours had twin boys. I would not be surprised if more babies arrive this summer. By this I mean, several women who are thin like everyone else have big, round bellies.

It is odd, but I am more patient these days, even around crying children. I have not yelled at Sally in a while, nor have I stomped my foot when frustrated (though I should like to do so many times over!). Esther is a good influence on me. I like being friends with a married girl my age.

An express rider came through camp this afternoon. His poor horse was covered with clay as the roads are a river of sticky mud. General

Washington nearly wept with delight and relief upon hearing the news: His friend Lafayette has arrived safely in Boston! He came aboard a fast frigate by the King's favor, and the French fleet is near our shores.

This journey to France and back took Lafayette one full year and three months.

Another day

From the new paper Willie gave me, I made four little books. With a nail and a rock, I hammered holes along one side, wove a thin leather strap through the holes, then tied a knot. This fastened the pages together. Now my young students — Sally, Mazie, Anna, and Robert — each have a journal for their lessons. And we have two quills between us, so when one child is writing words, the other is reading.

I'm not a good teacher. I do not know how to make Robert behave. When I ask him to please stop poking his sister, he does, but only for a moment. Soon he is wiggling again and making rude noises with his mouth. Anna and Mazie pay attention to their lessons, but Sally keeps sighing as if she is exhausted. She wants to run outside and play. I *myself* want to run outside.

But Mrs. Campbell and Mama say that being at war is no excuse for not learning. Thus, I keep trying to teach what little I know. The children are writing stories.

Mazie read hers aloud. It went like this: "Mammy and Victor sit by the fire and talk. They are friends."

Anna's story was about her baby sister: "Betsy knows how to walk now. She likes the creek. I catch her before she falls in."

Robert wrote: "The drums are loud. The guns are louder. The cannons are loudest."

This was Sally's story: "I like dogs. I want to play with one."

May 10, 1780, Wednesday

The rolling hills around Jockey Hollow are green with patches of wildflowers. Yesterday after our lessons, the girls and I put away our journals then dashed out of the hut. Robert came, too. We ran through fields, over a creek, and up a slope. We just felt like running! When we reached Headquarters, we heard a commotion coming along the road. Horsemen and soldiers were cheering.

"Lafayette!" came the shouts. "Huzzah! Huzzah!"

We each jumped upon a tree stump, hoping to see him. But we glimpsed only the back of his light blue coat as he went into Headquarters.

This evening around the fire, we learned Lafayette has a terrible cold. Lady Washington has confined him upstairs, to a guest room across the hall from hers. She is fussing and caring for him. He is near the age of her son, Jacky.

May 19, 1780, Friday

An eerie darkness has fallen upon Jockey Hollow. It is almost noon and I am sitting outside on a rock, a candle by my side so I can see these words. People are walking among the huts with lanterns as if it is midnight, but we have not even had our noon meal.

There are no clouds in the sky. No stars or

moon. No sun. Just an inky blackness. We cannot do chores except to cook over our fire. I must go help Mama.

Next day

At dawn this morning, shouts echoed through Jockey Hollow. The sun was rising! It had not disappeared forever as many of us had worried.

May 1780 — not sure of the date

There has been some bad news:

Some weeks ago, the British seized Charleston, South Carolina. The Americans were forced to surrender to Generals Clinton and Cornwallis. All our equipment, cannons, and ships anchored there were lost to the enemy.

"'Tis one of our worst defeats of this war," Papa told us. "We are losing the South."

At the time, the French were still sailing across the Atlantic. They were too far away to help.

We have also learned that the darkness on May 19 happened throughout New England. During that long day, villagers worked by candlelight while their hens roosted and the whip-poor-wills sang their night serenades. No one can explain this strange event.

June 5, 1780, Monday

British and Hessian soldiers, many thousands of them, are marching through the American colonies like droves of ants. They are taking over!

In New Jersey they are burning homes and have ruined the village of Springfield. They shot cows, leaving them to rot, and then they murdered a minister's wife. A young Patriot named Jacob Ford was wounded there. He is the eldest son of Mrs. Ford, whose mansion sheltered Mazie and me during that blizzard. The other day when I was near Headquarters, a wagon carrying Jacob arrived. Mrs. Ford rushed out, calling his name. His uniform was bloody. As the men carried him inside I could see that he was just a boy, barely old enough to fire his own musket.

General Washington has ordered the Army to be ready to march at any moment. We know not where. Lady Washington and the officers' wives are packing, and so are we. We have been in Jockey Hollow for six months.

After Papa and Willie readied their gear, they came to say good-bye, with Thomas and Victor. It's so sudden! We shall be following them with the baggage, but they might end up wounded. I am nervous! I worry also for Thomas and the other boys who play music for the marching soldiers.

When Victor and Miss Lulu walked to the creek for a private moment, Willie came over to me. He still has no hat to shade his face. "We'll be cooking on our own while on the march, but I shall look for you, Abby. I'll miss your soup that tastes like a shirt."

"And I shall miss your compliments, Willie."

Johnny wears his own tricorn that Mrs. Campbell sewed for him. When he saluted Papa and the others, he was such a brave little fellow I swallowed hard not to cry.

After a three-day march

I hate the Army. I hate this war.

After starting our cooking fire, I went for a walk with my friend Esther. She wanted to find her husband and I hoped to see Willie. When we came around a bend in the road there was a small hill with a tree. A dead soldier was hanging from a high limb. His hat and one of his shoes had fallen to the dirt.

When we recognized the purple face, we clung to each other. It was a horrible sight. We had seen him among the Pennsylvania troops.

"What did he do?" Esther cried.

I remembered Valley Forge. "Mutiny?" I wondered aloud. "Or perhaps he stole from an officer?"

Just then two dragoons rode by on horseback, tall in their saddles. Their sabers shone in the sunlight.

"He was a spy," one of the men volunteered. "Our Army is infested with them. They pretend to be Patriots, but then they report to the British. Careful who you talk to, girls."

I glanced at the fallen tricorn and decided not to pick it up. It was not worthy of Willie Campbell.

July 15, 1780, Saturday

Yesterday a woman next to us collapsed while scrubbing clothes at the riverbank. Her face and neck were so sunburned, we carried her into the shade. She came to when we cooled her off with wet rags, but an hour later she stopped breathing. There was naught we could do to save her.

It wrenched my heart to hear the wailing of her three young daughters. Their Papa came from his brigade to comfort them. He has asked another family to please care for them until he can be discharged.

Now we are more careful in this heat. Most of us have woven straw hats to shade our faces, and we drink water whenever we can to keep from fainting. I worry about Willie and the other soldiers being out in the sun all day.

I do love summer, though. When it doesn't rain we sleep outside to watch the stars. During the day we can bathe ourselves in the creeks and our laundry dries fast in the hot sun. Mosquitoes are torture, but I will gladly suffer them any day over a blizzard.

July 19, 1780, Wednesday

This morning, messengers brought good news:

The French have finally arrived in Rhode Island! Their many ships are crowding the bay of Newport. The soldiers — someone said there are 5,000 — are well-fed and wearing clean white uniforms with snappy hats. They set up tents on one of the islands that the enemy had just evacuated. Now General Washington is relaying messages to their commander, Count de Rochambeau. They have translators.

All pray they will help rid our country of the Redcoats.

On one of our walks, Esther and I discovered an orchard with apples and walnuts. The farmhouse had burned down, only the chimney stood. With charcoal, someone had written on the stones, "Death to Tories! All Loyalists go back to England!"

We found the remains of a porcelain doll in the ashes. I thought of Sally. In my mind I could see a little girl who lost her home then had to sail across the ocean without her doll.

July 31, 1780, Monday

New York, near West Point. We are camped with women from the Pennsylvania Brigade. Many are nurses for the men who are ill or wounded. All of us help with washing, mending, and cooking.

We abandoned our heavy iron kettles in Jockey Hollow and now use ones made of tin, issued to us by the quartermaster. They are much lighter to carry. Our washtubs also are tin. Now with one pot for cooking and one for laundry, I hope our soup tastes better!

This month four babies were born. None have died yet. I think hot weather is easier for the little ones to bear than the winter cold. Still no letter from Elisabeth. Mama is beginning to worry.

Rations are so scarce the regiments have been going out in small detachments, to hunt and to find food in the countryside. Some farmers are glad to share, but most are tired of this war — now six long years — and they demand payment. Our soldiers have no money. If no one is at home, they walk into barns and pantries, taking what they can to keep from starving. They grab shirts hanging from hooks and shoes placed under beds, to replace their ragged uniforms.

Yesterday Papa told us he and Victor found a rooster on a fence. They trapped it, wrung its neck, and plucked its feathers. Then they walked into the nearest farmhouse without knocking on the door, praying that it was not the home of Tories.

"Please may we use your fire?" Victor asked the lady. When she nodded, they put the rooster on a spit and sat by the flames until it had cooked. They were so starved they ate it right then, the sizzling hot fat burning their tongues and lips.

"Forgive us, madam," Papa said. "We have nothing to pay for your kindness." To their surprise, she gave them two live hens in a sack.

"Hurry away from here," she told them, "before my husband returns from the village."

Last night Miss Lulu made a delicious soup from those chickens, with walnuts and dandelions.

When the men come into camp, they tell stories similar to Papa's. Everyone is hungry all the time. The Army is desperate for supplies. General Washington has ordered the Army to stop raiding the countryside, but he is not punishing anyone who does.

Mama has lines in her face I had not noticed before. I wonder if I look weary as well. Knowing that Papa and Willie are stealing to survive pains us greatly.

"Why stay you in this wretched Army?" we asked.

"Freedom is coming," Papa answered.

Willie agreed. "Abby, we want a future without tyranny."

August 4, 1780, Friday

Rain. Our tent leaks. I did not sleep last night for the mud oozing under my back. This morning when Willie saw that I was shivering, he brought his blanket to warm me.

I felt a little shy with his arm around me, but did not squirm away. "Thank you," I said.

"You're welcome, Abby. The days don't seem so long when you're beside me."

August 13, 1780, Sunday

Church under the trees this morning. In the middle of a hymn, I realized Johnny was missing and so was his playmate, Betsy Ewing. She is the little sister of Anna and Robert. For half the day we searched in a panic. Finally we found them under a pine tree, sound asleep. They were hidden by the low branches. Such was their slumber in this heavy heat, they had not heard us screaming their names.

Mama did not scold me for losing sight of my brother — during church all of us had been praying with our eyes closed.

We have learned that ten days ago General Washington gave Benedict Arnold a high honour: the command of West Point. This fort juts out into the Hudson, where there is a narrow S curve. Large vessels must slow down to navigate the turn, which allows our cannons and artillery to fire before being fired upon. Also to stop the British warships, there is an iron chain across the river. One end is anchored on Constitution Island, the other on the opposite shore. Log rafts attached to the chain keep it from sinking, and anchors keep it from drifting in the strong current.

"Each link is the size of Johnny," Mr. Campbell said, holding his hand over my brother's head. "About two feet long, and thick as this boy's leg. How about that?" He and other blacksmiths want to repair some weak spots, he told us, but General Arnold will not give his approval. They do not know why.

"'Tis most troubling," said Mr. Campbell.

September 22, 1780, Friday

This afternoon at sunset, Willie, Papa, and Victor ran into camp. They were out of breath and faint from the heat. They had not eaten for two days. Right away, Miss Lulu sat them down with a cup of mushroom broth and a piece of her honey cake.

"An English warship is down near Stony Point," Willie told us. "'Tis the sloop *Vulture*. I saw the name painted on her stern. Our troops fired, forcing her downriver. But all hands were on deck and not a bit afraid. I'd say, if the wind turns in her favor she shall return under the cover of darkness."

"Papa, what does this mean?" I asked.

"'Tis not good," he said. "Our enemies want to capture West Point. If they succeed, they shall control the Hudson River, from Albany all the way down to the ocean where New York Harbor is."

"What then, Papa?"

He swallowed the last of his broth then stood to shoulder his musket. "The British Navy will own the Hudson, slicing us in two with their warships."

September 23, 1780, Saturday

Esther and I were emptying a washtub into the brush when a messenger rode through camp. He reported disturbing news:

An Englishman in simple clothing was stopped on the road near Tarrytown. Our guards questioned then searched him. When they found six papers in his boot describing the weaknesses of West Point, they realized he was a spy. He tried to bribe them with his horse and his watch to let him go, but they still took him to Headquarters in

Tappan. His true identity is Major John André. It seems those papers were written by a high-ranking officer in our Army who is planning to defect to the British.

September 29, 1780, Friday

All of us in camp were eager to hear about Major André's trial in Tappan. It was held today at Headquarters. We wanted to know who the American traitor is, and if harm has come to our Army. The story is this:

John André sailed up the Hudson aboard the *Vulture*, which anchored below Stony Point. In the middle of the night he rowed to shore, for a prearranged meeting in the forest. Someone gave him the damning papers, but at his trial he would not say who.

He is to be hanged in three days.

After we heard this news, Esther and I went looking in the woods for apples. Her striped dress is ragged along the hem like mine and she has gone barefoot these warm months to save her shoes. Her feet are brown from the sun. As we walked, she told me two interesting things. One was a story about Major John André.

"When the British occupied Philadelphia, he lived next door to us in Benjamin Franklin's house. That was two winters ago," she explained. "He's a charming gent, an artist, and he speaks several languages. He drew a picture of me with my cat."

"Do you think he is truly a spy?" I asked.

"That I don't know," she said. "But I *do* know he took some of Mr. Franklin's belongings without permission. The cook told me he put a pen knife and an ivory comb into the cuff of his coat sleeve when he left the city."

The other interesting thing Esther told me is that she is expecting a baby!

September 30, 1780, Saturday

Distress. I write these words with panic in my heart. Johnny and Betsy Ewing have been missing all morning. They were playing at my side while I was grinding coffee beans. I turned to look for a heavier rock, but when I came back they were gone.

They are not in anyone's tent and they are not under any tree. Everyone is searching for their footprints in the soft dirt. I am sick with worry.

Still Saturday—rainstorm

Sally and I are by the fire, trying to dry off. Thunder is still rumbling in the distance and the earth is muddy. The rain stopped, but it washed away all signs of where Johnny and Betsy might have walked. How will we ever find them now?

Miss Lulu is making each of us drink a cup of hot broth for nourishment. There is no honey cake today. All the mothers and children are taking turns searching, then warming themselves while others go out to look.

Still Saturday—late afternoon

The sun will set in an hour! Already shadows in the woods are dark, and still we have not found Betsy or my little brother. Mama keeps pressing her hand to her heart as if to quiet its pounding. If only we could make time stop and go back to this morning. I would have tied those two babies to my wrist.

Mrs. Ewing is keeping Anna and Robert by her skirts.

"Please God, not another one," she cried. She told Mama that she has lost two children to small pox, one to measles. "Betsy is our little angel. God gave her to us to heal our heartbreak. I don't know what I'll do—"

Mama hugged her.

"There, there, ladies," said Miss Lulu, trying to comfort them. "I am prayin' for those dear little ones. Hang on."

Still Saturday—night

Papa and Willie are searching with Mr. Ewing along the creeks with torches. So are Victor and Mr. Campbell, but in the opposite direction. Thomas is here by the fire. Though he is just eleven years of age, he patted my hand to comfort me. I keep forgetting that he has suffered the loss of his parents.

All of us are drowsy but cannot sleep. Fear is eating at my stomach.

October 1, 1780, Sunday—dawn

The worst has happened.

I am looking out our tent at a mist rising through the woods. Shouts just came from across the creek. Someone has found a child's body.

Still Sunday—noon

Victor came into camp, two babes in his arms. Betsy's golden hair was dripping. It looked white against his black skin. My heart raced when I saw Johnny's sopping shirt.

Mama and Mrs. Ewing cried out, weeping at the sight.

But Victor shouted, "Ma'am, this one's breathin'!"

I shall forever rejoice that my brother lives. Victor found him on a sandbar, soaked and shivering inside a tangle of driftwood. Betsy was floating facedown in an eddy.

We do not know what happened. It seems they went to the creek to play, all in the instant that I turned my back. Johnny does not know how to swim, so he must have waded over to the sand-bar—the water is shallow enough.

Why his sweet little friend drowned, yet he did not, I shall never understand. It was not for lack of a mother's fervent prayers.

October 2, 1780, Monday

This morning Willie and young Thomas made a small coffin from slabs of bark they gathered in the forest.

Mrs. Ewing came to me. "'Tis not your fault, Abigail dear. Our Betsy was always running off. Now she's in Heaven with my other children. Some day I shall see them again." When Mrs. Ewing put her arms around me, I wept like a baby. I thought my heart would burst.

Just before sunset a horseman brought news into camp, but we were too spent to ask questions. All we know is that Major John André was hanged today. And that the American traitor is Benedict Arnold.

October 6, 1780, Friday

The heat of summer is gone. My thoughts are heavy, remembering little Betsy. Though her mother does not blame me, I cannot ease this heartache. If only I had kept better watch.

Days are cool as the leaves change color and fall into swirling piles. Soon the Army shall march to winter camps. Many of the women will follow their husbands to West Point where General Washington had his Headquarters last year. More shall winter in Burlington, others near Boston. Our family and new friends are returning to Jockey Hollow with the Pennsylvania line — about 2,000 soldiers.

We are learning more about General Arnold:

For many months he has been sending secret codes to the enemy about our troops, our locations, and our artillery. He was to be paid handsomely — thousands of pounds — and given a command in the Royal Army if he succeeded in turning over West Point to the British. It was he who wrote the papers hidden in Major André's boot.

When told that the major had been arrested,

Benedict Arnold left his young wife and baby in his quarters at West Point and ran to shore. A bargeman rowed him downriver to the *Vulture*, thus he escaped. His wife, Peggy, was a Loyalist and in on the plot.

General Washington was stunned when informed of this treachery.

"He was beside himself," the messenger told us. "Later, I was in a tavern with him. His aides urged him to join them at the table with their maps, but he would not. His Excellency paced back and forth in the barroom, holding a bowl of milk, too upset to drink it. His face was red with fury."

How much damage has been done to the Continental Army, no one yet knows. At least West Point did not fall into the hands of the British.

I wonder if Peggy will be executed like Major André.

October 9, 1780, Monday

Johnny has a deep cough from being on the sand-bar all night in wet clothes. Mrs. Campbell and

Miss Lulu help Mama by taking turns holding him. They wrap him in a blanket with a heated rock upon his chest.

We are praying for him. Also we are praying that God bring comfort to Betsy's family. Anna is so heartsore she will not go near the creek, not even to fetch water. I am trying to keep the children busy with reading and writing, but for now they are not interested in school.

I deserve to be shunned, but the Ewings are not doing so. I am humbled by their graciousness.

December 25, 1780, Monday

Jockey Hollow, New Jersey. Two months have passed since I last opened these pages. We have been consumed caring for Johnny's pneumonia. At last his cough is gone, but suddenly it's Christmas!

This morning Thomas came to our hut with gifts. He is taller by the month, and now has freckles across his nose. His red hair was tied back in a queue like the older men.

"Merry Christmas!" he said.

For us ladies, he had made a beautiful wreath of

pine to hang on our wall. Woven into the branches were sprigs of holly and some golden leaves left over from autumn. Its fresh aroma sweetened our crowded cabin.

"Thomas dear, how very thoughtful of you," said Mama.

He then held out a little drum he had made, with two sticks. "Johnny lad, this is for you. Your very own, as I promised when you were ailing."

"Tom, thank you! I like drums!"

Ow, our ears! The noise from a three-year-old with a banging toy is painful. After some minutes Mama said, "Johnny, we shall rest your drum for now. You have a very important job — to announce supper for everyone."

That is how Mama got my brother to make his noise just once a day.

We are in a different shelter from last year. While we were gone during the summer, many of the huts were torn down by the farmers. They needed the logs to rebuild the fences that our soldiers had taken for firewood. Still, Jockey Hollow looks like a little village with rows of cabins and muddy paths in between.

The weather is not as cruel this December, though food is still scarce. Mama is so thin, her cheeks have shadows.

I read back in this diary to remember a merry Christmas in Valley Forge, before our house burned. I had a stomachache from drinking too much Egg Nog, and did not like the scarf Elisabeth had knit me. I was such a child.

This is now our second year of following Papa and the Army.

I think of my dear friends back home, but their faces are becoming pale memories.

December 27, 1780, Wednesday

I am feeling sorry for myself today.

I do not care about silk or satin, but how I would love some new clothes. My sleeves and apron are dotted black from sparks off the cooking fire — soon the cotton will shred from so many holes. The strings on my cap have rotted. I need one that won't blow off in the wind, and I would love new shoes as well. My feet are always wet, always cold.

But when I see the other girls and mothers in rags, the soldiers with bare legs, I feel ashamed. All of us are in need.

Every day after the men drill and clean artillery, Willie comes calling. He is nearly nineteen now and has the handsome face of his father.

First he greets his mother with a kiss then he says, "Miss Abigail, will you do me the honour?"

We walk to the edge of the forest and up a small hill where we dust the snow off a tree stump. There we sit. It's too cold to be out for long. We chat until we start shivering, then he offers his arm so I won't slip on the icy path.

"Careful, Abby," he always says.

But today when I took his arm, instead of watching my step, I glanced up at his face. He is a fine-looking boy. That instant, my feet slid out from under me and down I went, pulling him with me. We slid on our rumps to the bottom of the hill.

"Whoops!" we both said, laughing. His new tricorn, given to him by the quartermaster, bounced from his head and slid with us in the snow.

Now I know why I want a new dress. It's because

of Willie Campbell. Being with him makes me want to look pretty.

December 28, 1780, Thursday

Once again the soldiers are talking mutiny. While Mama and the other women pleaded with them to stay in camp, we served them ash-cake — this is just flour and water mixed together on a rock then thrown in the ashes to bake. It has a bitter, grainy taste but it was their supper. The men devoured it with cups of hot coffee.

"Husbands, *please*," said Mrs. Campbell. "They execute spies and mutineers. You could all be hanged!" Though her husband is a blacksmith for the troops, he, too, is ready to take up arms on behalf of the men.

"Pardon me, ladies, but we are practically skeletons. Look." One of the soldiers lifted his shirt to show his ribs. "If Congress wants us to fight the enemy, they must put *something* in our bellies. We cannot keep eating the bark off trees."

"We have not been paid in months," my father reminded everyone.

"And for many of us," said Mr. Ewing, "our three-year enlistments are expiring. They cannot force us to stay in this misery."

Mama pulled me away from the campfire. We hurried back to our hut. The men's voices were low and rumbling, like something about to happen.

Still Thursday, late at night

Before bed, we looked out the door. In the darkness we could see candlelight among clusters of men. They were talking in small groups, walking around camp, meeting with others.

Mama brushed my hair in long, quiet strokes, then plaited it. I am old enough to do this myself, but I like being close to her. And I like being close to Sally. She sat in my lap while I plaited *her* hair, and *she* plaited Mazie's five pigtails.

"What will we do if there's a mutiny?" I asked no one in particular. I could see Miss Lulu and Mrs. Campbell exchange looks, and I could feel Mama behind me taking a deep breath.

"We have spoken to some of the other wives,"

she answered. "Many of us are going to follow our husbands."

Mrs. Campbell nodded. "If anything happens to our men, we want to know about it. We want to be there."

"That's right," said Miss Lulu.

"But where are the soldiers going?" asked Sally. "Is it far? What will they do?"

"They are taking their complaints to Congress, Sally dear. Philadelphia is perhaps a three-day march, that is, if there are no blizzards."

Sally jumped up. "Elisabeth is in Philadelphia. We can see our new baby!"

A look of worry came into my mother's eyes. She knows I have written many letters to my sister. We are distressed by her lack of response. "I dream of that day," Mama said, "when we can all be together again."

New Year's Eve, 1780

It is late. I am by the fire to keep warm. Throughout the Pennsylvania camp, men are shouting and cheering, welcoming the New Year. But we in our hut are quiet. We know another reason they celebrate.

Tomorrow eleven regiments will desert their posts!

New Year's Day, 1781, Monday

We can hear the clatter of muskets being shouldered and footsteps from hundreds and hundreds of soldiers lining up to leave Jockey Hollow. There is jangling of harnesses from the horses hitched to cannons and baggage wagons.

Gunshots are frightening us. Captain Bitting was killed trying to stop the mutiny. We saw his body sprawled in a puddle of red snow. Several others were wounded. We watched Captain Tolbert go down, bleeding from the throat. Men carried him into a hut but if he lived or died, we do not know.

General Wayne is urging his troops to stay, to no effect. Now drummers are calling the soldiers, and the march has begun. Our Thomas is going with them! The *rat-a-tat-tats* echo through this cold valley. The fifers sound like birds tweeting.

I looked for Willie, but saw only rows of men in

ragged coats and tricorns, moving down the road. Now I must hurry. . . .

Near Middlebrook, New Jersey

Evening. We are on the outskirts of the army encampment with other women who followed the soldiers. Twelve of us are crowded into one tent, but we are in good company: Esther and her mother, and Mrs. Ewing with Robert and Anna. There is so little space that last night we slept sitting up and leaning against one another.

Today our walk was in slippery snow through shaded woods. It was cold. We were exhausted before the sun even touched the tops of the trees. Esther told me she had stomach pains and her back hurt. It was hard for her to stand up. I asked one of the wagon drivers if my friend could please ride for a bit, but he said no, that if he let *her* climb aboard he would have *all* the ladies asking.

By sunset Esther was crying in agony.

I had forgotten my friend was expecting a baby because she never spoke of it and her cape covers her well. But just an hour ago there it was, right before our eyes! A tiny little girl she named Polly. We are all smiling, the first any of us have done so in days.

January 7, 1781, Sunday

Princeton, New Jersey. The mutineers have captured this town! We hear the news as it makes its way down the line to our tents.

Here it is: The soldiers are not continuing to Philadelphia after all. They have set up headquarters here and have appointed envoys. They want to negotiate with General Wayne, who has followed the troops here. He could have everyone court-martialed, if he so ordered.

And there is more trouble coming.

This morning Sally and I were breaking ice at the creek, for water to boil, when two horsemen rode by. One appeared to be a local villager guiding an Englishman into the encampment. They came so close to where we were kneeling, we could smell the talc and grease from the Englishman's powdered wig. He looked regal in his crimson coat, clean white breeches, and boots freshly polished.

When he dismounted to talk to a group of our soldiers, Sally and I crept among the trees to listen.

"Back wages and all the victuals you can eat," he told them. "And a full pardon. King George won't have you hanged for being the piggish rebels you are."

The Americans crossed their arms, regarding him with scorn. "Eh, mate, all this good fortune in exchange for what?"

"Come to our side. You shall help the King end this silly war once and for all."

"Who sent you here?" demanded one of the Americans.

The man stood tall, his hand on his sword. "Sir Henry Clinton," he answered with pride. "British Commander in Chief for North America, resident of New York City. He knows of your hunger, you wretched misguided lads."

Sally and I were silent. We waited until the Englishman returned to his horse then ran back to the tents. We told the ladies what we had heard.

Later, still Sunday, January 7

Many of the wives worry this mutiny shall end in disaster, and that General Washington will never be able to restore order among the troops.

"Starving men will do anything to survive," warned one of the women. "Some of my uncles and cousins have thrown down their arms to march with the British, they are that destitute."

Mama clenched her fist. "*My* husband shall never betray our country," she boasted of my father. "He is no Benedict Arnold."

"Nor mine. Nor my son," said Mrs. Campbell. Mrs. Ewing agreed, saying, "Our husbands are Patriots. *We* are Patriots. We have come too far and lost too much to give up now."

I lowered my eyes in shame. Mrs. Ewing meant the loss of her little Betsy.

Then Miss Lulu told us something about Victor. He had been one of Captain Todd's slaves, but Captain Todd freed him when he joined the Army and deeded fifty acres of land to him.

"Victor can farm after this war," Miss Lulu explained. "We gonna see that pretty day, I jess know it. That fine man won't trade his blue coat for a red one, nosir."

Still Sunday, January 7

The mutineers' cannons are rolling into formation. We fear a bloody battle.

"Take the little ones," Mama instructed us. "Run far, far back."

Now from our tent I can see some of our Continentals lining up, muskets pointed. I want to see more! Where is Papa? Where is Willie?

Esther is here with her new baby. "Go, Abby! I shall watch these young ones. Then tell me if you have seen my husband. Hurry!"

I did not see Papa or the others when I drew near the cannons. Men were about to light the long cotton fuses when a shout rose from their ranks.

"Hold your fire!"

When they put down their torches, women standing nearby shouted questions.

One of the men tried to explain. "We wanted

to give Joseph Reed a cannon salute, to honour him but—"

"*Who?*" they interrupted.

"The President of Congress. He's come from Philadelphia to hear our grievances."

Another wife yelled, "Then welcome him with a hearty round, boys!"

"Woman," he hollered, "we realized firing artillery would scare the locals. Now go back to your laundry or whatever dirty chore you do."

January 8, 1781, Monday

Our sentries have seized the Englishman and his guide, and turned them over to General Wayne. We heard they are to be shot by a firing squad.

Mama and her friends were right. Our men have refused to accept the bribes from Sir Henry Clinton. In the quiet of my heart, I knew Willie would be steadfast.

And this morning, a happy event cheered us further. Villagers slaughtered several cows then delivered chunks of beef to our campfires. Supper is soon. The delicious aroma of roasting meat quickens my hunger.

Monday evening, after cleaning pots

When I filled Willie's plate with our good, hot stew, he insisted I share with him. "Come sit beside me, Abby. You are looking too thin. I worry about you."

"I'm fine, Willie."

He handed me his spoon. "Then let's sup together, and visit. I like the sound of your voice."

I sat in the dirt beside him, full of questions. "What if there had been a battle today?"

"I'm a soldier, Abby."

"But what if you got wounded?"

Willie grinned at me. "I would've bled all over the place."

"Then what?" I asked.

"Well, I guess I would've needed you to nurse me back to health."

Now that it is nightfall and I'm back in the ladies' camp, I think that dear fellow might enjoy some silence. How we chatted and chatted! I do hope he's not weary of me. I should like to have more conversations with him.

January 10, 1781, Wednesday

Full moon. It is bright and frosty tonight. I am able to write in this crowded tent by the glowing canvas. I shall be brief as my fingers are numb with cold.

An agreement was reached today, among the Continentals, General Wayne, and Joseph Reed. Letters from General Washington entered the discussions.

To our great relief, no mutineers will be hanged.

Half of our men have accepted honourable discharges and shall return to their homes. The other half will take furloughs. If they reenlist in April, they shall receive bonuses and become the new Pennsylvania Battalion.

Papa and Willie are in this latter group, as are Victor and our other friends.

I am glad Esther and I can spend more time together. I like her, and I like her little Polly, now ten days old. We walk together through camp gathering rags for diapers. Mrs. Campbell sewed a snug little bag for Polly to fit in. Now Esther can carry her close to her chest while keeping her hands free. We take turns. When holding her baby, I feel calm.

This morning a horseman brought distressing news. All of us hoped Benedict Arnold would be captured and hanged as a traitor. But he is alive, eating well, and waving the British flag. Just days ago he led a naval expedition that burned Richmond, Virginia. He has joined the enemy and is the enemy!

His wife, Peggy, is safe, too. Instead of putting her in prison, General Washington sent her to Philadelphia to live with her father, a Tory who is loyal to the King.

Tories are everywhere! My sister Elisabeth might well be a neighbour to one. I cannot bear the thought.

January 29, 1781, Monday

The Pennsylvania line has shrunk. Only eleven hundred men remain. At least that many are now walking through the snow back to their farms and villages. Their revolt was such a success that New Jersey troops tried the same thing.

A light snow was falling as a messenger told us what happened. He stayed in his saddle, his blue cloak turning white. I could hear the hiss of snowflakes drifting onto our shoulders as he spoke:

"About two hundred of 'em marched to Trenton," he said. "But General Washington has had enough of mutinies. He sent troops from West Point to restore order and had the leaders arrested. Two were sentenced to death."

"Have ye names, sir?" asked a woman standing with us. "My brothers are with the New Jersey line."

"Were they hanged?" another asked.

"Don't know who they were, ladies. I'm sorry. They were put before a firing squad made up of their own brigade. Their weeping companions were forced to shoot them."

April 24, 1781, Tuesday

For three months I have been without ink for my pen, thus this long silence. The latest news is troubling:

· The British have raided General Washington's home in Mount Vernon! They sailed up the Potomac and anchored near shore. Fortunately the General was not there, otherwise he would have been taken prisoner. But his cousin Lund Washington, who was in charge of the plantation, went aboard the enemy vessels and served refreshments. Then to continue his hospitality, he gave away several Negroes!

"The General is furious," the messenger reported, standing in the back of a wagon so his voice would carry.

A murmur of sympathy rose among us. Miss Lulu was next to me. She called out a question. "Kind sir, who was taken? Do you know names?"

He squinted, trying to remember. "Alls I heard is, three of the general's favorite old servants, also the lads Thomas and Peter, Gunner the bricklayer, Watty the weaver, and three young maids. Maybe they were given away, maybe they deserted. 'Tis not my concern. They're property of the enemy now."

Miss Lulu closed her eyes. A small cry escaped her lips.

"What's wrong, Miss Lulu?" I asked.

"That's my Pappy, Gunner the bricklayer. Our master sold 'im when I was little-bitty. I coulda died of lonesomeness. Now I ain't never gonna see him again."

I wanted to comfort Miss Lulu. I did not know how, except to stand beside her and be quiet.

Warmer days

Rations are still low, but there are plenty of ducks and geese near shore. They are nesting. It is not easy to catch a goose, for the big males charge us with flapping wings. While they honk and snap, one of us hurries to scare the female and wring her neck. I am sorry for the babies ready to hatch, but we are hungry.

May 7, 1781, Monday

Near West Point, spring. The moon is full and beautiful tonight. Finally the tall drifts of snow have melted and we are able to bathe in the creeks. As I write this in our tent, I am savoring this past hour spent with Willie. I cannot sleep.

After supper he and I strolled by the river. I was pondering how everyone is gaining years during this long war so I asked his age. He thought a moment.

"Uh . . . twenty? Yes, that's it. I am twenty now. You?"

"Fifteen."

"Abby, perhaps we should have a party for all our missed birthdays."

"Yes!" I replied. "And Miss Lulu can make her honey cake."

Willie fell quiet. He took my hand as we continued along the moonlit bank. Water swished against the tall reeds growing there. "There's something else I should like to celebrate with you," he said.

I felt my heart beat a bit faster. "Oh?" I said. "That I no longer cook soup in our laundry kettle?"

He laughed. "Abigail, I have known for a very long time that I want to marry you. You make me happy. I want to make you happy as well."

"Truly?"

"Yes, truly," he said.

"But the war—"

"Doesn't matter." He looked up at the bright sky. "It might go on for years, more than I am willing to wait. Please say yes, Abby. We can wed on the next full moon. Already I have asked your father for your hand."

"*You did?* When? What did he say?"

By way of an answer, Willie put his arms around me. I let him hold me. No longer did I feel shy.

Now I shall close these pages and tell Mama. But I think she already knows. She has set down her knitting. In the glow of her candle, I can see that she is giving me a tender look.

I shall not tell her about our kisses, though. The first one was quick. The second one . . . well, I shall keep the words to myself lest Sally peek in these pages.

A new family

A quiet, little wedding yesterday, but not my own. Victor and Miss Lulu were married at sunset, by one of the army chaplains. Their contentment touched me. Mazie leaned into Victor's arms like he was her own Papa.

During the ceremony Willie and I kept glancing at each other. I believe he will be an honourable husband, but dear me, I know nothing about being a wife — and our wedding is just weeks away!

May 13, 1781, Sunday

Still near West Point. Headquarters are in New Windsor, just north of West Point. Today a horseman brought news into camp: General Washington is speaking with the French commander, Count de Rochambeau. Our two armies shall meet up with his, then together all will head south to Virginia, where more Continentals are waiting. We will then battle the British that are there causing trouble.

"When shall this be?" a woman asked.

"Do the families follow this time?" another wanted to know.

"Exactly where is the Army going?"

The messenger held up his hand for quiet, then said, "The Brits in Virginia have been burning warehouses of tobacco, and destroying boats in the docks. Governor Thomas Jefferson is furious. So ladies, be ready to leave at a moment's notice. I'm under orders to say no more." He rode away without answering our questions.

"Why can't he tell us?" asked Sally.

"General Washington is smart," Mama explained. "Perhaps he knows how we ladies like to visit with one another. If we describe to a friend specifically where our Army is going, she will tell *her* friend who might tell a neighbour. That neighbour would tell a Tory, who would then tell a British officer. Before long, the enemy would know everything General Washington is planning."

Later when Sally and I were spreading blankets over bushes to air them out, she started to cry.

"Sally, what's wrong?"

"I'm scared for Mazie!" Then leaning close to me she whispered, "Abby, when we go south, what if their old master sees her and Miss Lulu? Or what if someone reads a poster about them running away? I mean, Tilda and Philomena running away."

I thought a moment. "Well, it's been a couple years. Maybe they don't look like they used to. Or maybe their master died in this war. Sally, all we can do is pray that they stay free."

My sister smiled up at me. "I like to pray," she said.

May 31, 1781, Thursday

A dreadful accident!

This morning from the cliff, Esther and I watched a barge crossing over to our side of the Hudson. There were about twenty people from Massachusetts: soldiers and women with children. Suddenly we heard screaming. Water was rushing up to their knees as the barge tipped from its heavy load. Then before our eyes all were dumped into the river. A wagon, two horses, babies, everyone.

I had not seen Willie for several days nor had Esther seen Ned, her husband, for their brigade has been out on patrol. When she and I noticed a soldier floating facedown in the swift current, we both cried out. There was another dead man, then another. We yelled, pointing down to the three bodies, but no one heard us. Like logs adrift, they soon disappeared around a bend in the river.

Esther and I clutched hands. We watched people jumping in to rescue children, boats rowing out to help. Somehow the women — in their heavy wet skirts — managed to keep their infants afloat. Men swam the horses to shore by holding on to their harnesses.

It was several hours before we learned that all had been saved except for those three. I am sad for their families.

Now it is evening. Campfires are glowing among the clusters of tents. We've been told that on the march south, there shall be many more river crossings. If we do indeed follow the Army, how I shall dread this.

June 2, 1781, Saturday

Days are sunny and warm, birds fill the trees with song. I'm feeling happy and hopeful. The ladies in camp got together and sewed a pretty wedding dress for me. The sleeves are of light blue linen, the skirt dark blue. My new mobcap was stitched from someone's apron, and they were able to find two shoes. One is brown, the other black, but they are of fine leather. I do feel elegant.

The moon will be full on Wednesday. I have whispered many questions to Esther about being married. She blushes as easily as do I. We would rather guess about some things than ask our mothers.

More than ever I miss my sister Elisabeth.

June 6, 1781, Wednesday

Today's chores shall keep me busy but I am thinking about this evening. The chaplain will be here at sunset.

The ladies made a bridal quilt. They sewed two blankets together like a pocket then filled it with soft downy feathers from geese and ducks. "This shall keep you and your husband warm in the woods," said Mrs. Ewing.

Husband! That word sounds strange when I say it.

Next day, sunrise

Camp is quiet this early hour. Willie helped me start a small fire for coffee; next I shall fry some bacon.

Last night, lanterns hanging from trees lighted our wedding dance. Supper was another celebration with friends and family toasting to our happiness. When Papa lifted his cup of cider, I noticed a tear on his cheek.

"I am not sad, Daughter," he later said, when I asked if he was all right. "You shall always be my little girl, but now Willie will take care of you."

I hear the coffee boiling — time to put down my quill and cook my first wifely breakfast. As I watch Willie bring more firewood, I am pondering my father's words.

June 8, 1781, Friday morning

An hour ago a soldier came into camp looking for Mrs. Campbell. I found her at the creek rinsing a pot.

"A messenger is here for you," I told her. We returned to the tents where a young orderly was holding a folded piece of paper.

"Is anything wrong?" she asked him. He gave her the letter and left.

Mrs. Campbell broke open the wax seal to read the message. She handed it to me, trying not to laugh. "Abby dear, this is for you. There are *two* Mrs. Campbells now."

"Oh!" I felt embarrassed. Willie and I were married two days ago, yet this is the first time I considered my new name. *Abby Campbell.* I like the sound of it.

Sally and Mazie were peering over my shoulder to see the letter; Mama and Miss Lulu were also wondering, so I read it aloud:

"'Dear Abigail, I have heard of your recent nuptials and should like to wish you well. Please join Mrs. Knox and me for tea this afternoon at Headquarters, three o'clock. Fond regards, Martha Washington.'"

Now it was *I* who smoothed my apron and looked at my hands. Suddenly I felt nervous. "I must brush my hair! Mother, is my face clean? Sally and Mazie, will you walk with me? If there are sweets, perhaps I can bring you each one."

We leave in a few minutes! I shall wear my new clothes as they are for every day now.

After tea with Lady Washington

The sunshine was warm so we girls did not need wraps. Sally and Mazie sat on a stone wall in front of Headquarters while I went inside. Mrs. Washington's parlour was cheerful with tall windows open to the fresh air. She smiled in greeting and motioned to a chair near hers.

"Sit by me, Abigail. Mrs. Knox, come join us now. You've helped me enough today."

Mrs. Knox swished over in her wide skirt. She set a tray on the table, with cookies and a teapot. "Hello again, Abby! I'm glad to see you. The last time we met, you had grown taller, and now you are married! How lovely. Congratulations, dear."

Words flew out of my mouth before I could think. "Thank you, ma'am. And I remember last time you were holding your new baby —" I stopped myself.

In the quiet that filled the room, Mrs. Knox poured our tea. The cup rattled in its saucer when she handed it to me. She said, "We lost Julia before her first birthday."

My mouth went dry. How could I have forgotten?!

"I am very sorry, Mrs. Knox. Julia was the prettiest baby." Ashamed of myself, I lowered my eyes. I'm trying to be a proper married lady, but in truth I am still just a girl. A girl with poor manners.

Lady Washington rescued me with friendly chat. "'Tis a brave calling to be the wife of a soldier," she said. "Take courage, Abby. We all help each other." Then she explained that she's been ill for two weeks and Mrs. Knox has been keeping her company.

"When do you return to Mount Vernon?" I asked.

"End of June, I pray. I miss my son, Jacky, and I have a new grandbaby to meet. Everyone worries the Redcoats might sail up the Potomac again and try to kidnap me. Bah. What would they want with an old woman? I am fifty. As army wives we must be brave, Abigail."

"Yes, ma'am."

When we had finished our tea she offered

the remaining cookies. "Dear, put these in your pocket, for your sister and her friend."

"Thank you, Lady Washington." This time when I curtsied good-bye, my skirt was long enough for a graceful sweep of the floor.

June 24, 1781, Sunday

I like church in the woods, but the mosquitoes and heat are torture. This morning the chaplain droned on so — God forgive me — I did not hear one word. Instead, I listened to the birds and the creek. With Willie beside me, I kept marveling, Here is my husband.

Some nights he is on guard duty for his battalion, but other nights we are able to be together. After supper we walk along the edge of camp where the cooking fires guide our way. He carries our quilt.

"Abby, when this war is over we shall return to Pennsylvania. We'll have a house of our own. No more sleeping in the forest."

July 17, 1781, Tuesday

Near West Point, New York. General Cornwallis and thousands of his Redcoats have seized Williamsburg, Virginia.

Our Army has now started its final campaign south. All of us are weary and hope this brings an end to the war. Cannons, artillery, soldiers, and ships are heading to Virginia. Women and baggage leave tomorrow at dawn. We will journey along many rivers.

We've been told there shall be a fierce battle. Where or when, we do not know. But one thing is certain: The British plan to reclaim our colonies for King George.

Yesterday when Willie lifted his musket to leave, I pretended to be brave. I did not cry. But after he marched away with all the men, I broke down weeping. In Valley Forge when we watched Papa go I was sad, yes, but I was just a girl of twelve. I knew so little.

Now nearly three years have passed. Willie is my husband. I cannot bear to think of anything happening to him. Why this is not the same as with Papa, I do not know. Perhaps fifteen is still too young to understand these things.

Early August 1781

Now Cornwallis and his troops are occupying Yorktown, Virginia.

Our soldiers are marching double time, to cover miles quickly, and are far ahead of us. We are noisy as we walk: babies cry, our kettles clang, stray dogs tag along. It is dreadfully hot, yet still, none of us are allowed to ride with the baggage. The wagons are so slow, we are able to jump in the creeks to cool off, then hurry back to the road before being left behind. In this heat I do not mind that my shift stays wet.

Johnny is a big boy now, three and a half. He walks with Sally and Mazie, I walk with Esther. When she is tired, I carry baby Polly. I keep thinking of Lady Washington, how she said soldiers' wives help each other.

Oh, to have her courage on this long journey. I do not want to see a battlefield.

. . . .

We have crossed into New Jersey and are heading toward the city of New York, where there are 10,000 Redcoats. The city is its own island, and beyond is Staten Island and Long Island. From a hill we can see British ships patrolling. Their tall, white sails make me think of swan feathers sharpened into pens. It is hard to imagine this harbor was frozen solid two winters ago, that our enemies could walk from shore to shore.

A horseman told us General Washington is going to attack, so our troops are settling in for a long siege. They are building rows of earthern ovens to bake bread — enough for our Army and the French who arrived under Rochambeau's command — also some redoubts and other fortifications.

We women have been ordered to set up tents here in the woods, and to be quiet. Mama and the others laughed at such an idea. Ladies rarely stop talking and children are never quiet.

August 8, 1781, Wednesday

When I did not eat any porridge this morning, Esther said, "Not hungry?"

I made a face. "No. I feel dreadful. All I want is to lie down and sleep. I pray I don't have typhoid or the Pox."

Esther felt my forehead. "No fever. Do your knees ache?"

"No."

"Does it pain you to swallow?"

"No."

She asked more questions, then put her hands on her hips. "Abby Campbell, you are not sick. You're going to have a baby!"

"What?"

"Yes." She counted on her fingers. "Probably next spring, in March."

"What?" I said again.

With the hem of her apron, Esther handed me a cup of steaming dandelion tea. "Drink this. 'Tis hot, but good for you. In a month or so you shall feel better, Abby. Don't worry. I'll help you."

A baby.

A few moments ago I went to the creek where

Mama was washing petticoats. "Mother, I'm expecting a child," I told her.

"I know, dear."

"You do? How?"

She leaned back on her heels to smile at me. "Abigail, some things a mother knows."

When alone in the woods where no one can see me, I rest my hand on my belly. A baby? I keep thinking, I, a mother? And I, not even a wife for two months? A quiet thrill leaves me in awe: I am carrying Willie's child.

Still August 1781

Near Trenton, New Jersey. No sooner had we set up our tents than we were told to strike them. Once again, we are on the move!

"Be quiet and be quick," an orderly instructed as we gathered our kettles and bags. He would not answer questions.

There has been no siege. There was no battle. There is no bread baking in those ovens. General Washington suddenly ordered our soldiers on a rapid march to the Delaware. At sunset they boarded ships and sailed downriver. Our troops are now in Philadelphia!

Their journey was overnight, but it shall take us three days of walking to meet up with them. We have suffered from much rain and are wet most of the time, even in our tents at night.

I write this by the campfire as we try to warm our blankets. My legs are tired. Johnny just collapsed in tears of exhaustion, poor little boy. Sally and Mazie have unraveled their braids to dry their hair. They twirl around and wave their arms to entertain us.

"Philadelphia!" Sally keeps saying.

September 3, 1781, Monday

Philadelphia. This is our last day here, in the home of Mrs. Darling. Captain greeted us with a wagging tail, jumping on Johnny and knocking him down. My sister Elisabeth cried with surprise. Her letters and ours must have been lost for she has been as worried about us as we were for her. She and Ben Valentine are well; their baby, Rose, is already walking.

Oh, to spend more time together, but we must join the rest of the women tomorrow morning at sunrise. Miss Lulu and Esther will hold up a flag of red ribbons so we can find them. Already, our troops are on their way south, and the French are marching through Philadelphia. Their long, white waistcoats are adorned with lapels in pink or green, yellow or sky blue. Sergeants have white plumes in their hats, chasseurs green, grenadiers red. A full band stepped with them, to cheering crowds, as they paraded past the Continental Congress. We are thrilled the French are here — thousands of them in a riot of colors — and there are many more aboard ships in the West Indies.

After six years of war, most of *our* soldiers are still without stockings. Though their coats are shabby, they are proud and cheerful. When the Pennsylvania Brigade marched by and I saw Papa, I yelled and waved to him, as did Sally and Mama.

But when Willie came around the corner I could not help myself. I ran to kiss his cheek. Many of the women did the same to their loved ones. Drums and fifes echoed through the stone streets, stirring me to tears. Young Thomas raised his sticks and twirled them in the air when he saw us jumping. He is taller than most of the boys now, his red hair in a long queue below his tricorn.

General Washington rode by on horseback, one hand holding the reins, the other rested near the hilt of his sword. His coat was buff and blue. He dipped his head to acknowledge the crowds, but did not smile.

"Godspeed!" we yelled. We ran alongside Willie's brigade to the harbor. They boarded a schooner loaded with gunpowder, to sail farther down the Delaware. Other vessels were at the docks to transport troops, including the French Commander Rochambeau. The greater part of the armies shall go by land. We will follow.

Before bed

Mrs. Darling's windows are open this warm evening. A full moon fills her parlour with light. Ben has been explaining what he heard from an officer yesterday: that General Washington has succeeded in tricking the enemy.

"All those ovens were a ruse," Ben told us during supper. "Their purpose was to make it *look* like the Americans and French would be settling in. It fooled ol' Clinton, the Redcoats' Commander in Chief there."

Ben Valentine leaned the stump of his arm on the table to hold down a sheet of paper. Then with his good hand, he sketched a map. "See, ladies, British ships are in New York Harbor ready to battle. But look." His pen dotted lines down the Delaware River to Philadelphia. "*Our* soldiers have safely sneaked away from the New York islands. General Washington has saved their strength and their powder for the South."

We stared at Ben's map. I felt a sudden hope for Willie and Papa, for the entire Continental Army.

Still September 3 — by Mrs. Darling's fire, unable to sleep

Moonlight is keeping me awake, also my stomach is knotted with worry — sunrise will be here in just a few hours! Some good news, though:

Admiral François de Grasse with his French fleet is sailing from the Caribbean toward the Chesapeake Capes—more than twenty ships with cannons and armed soldiers! We do not know when or how or where they will meet up with our Army. Lafayette is also leading troops in the South.

This house is quiet. I rocked Rosie to sleep in Mrs. Darling's chair, which still creaks and clicks like a clock. It is a marvel to me, to hold the child of my sister. I watched the little pink face in wonderment, realizing that in some months I shall be holding my own babe.

Other news for which I am grateful: Johnny and Sally will stay here. Elisabeth begged Mama and me not to go.

Mrs. Darling agreed. "You have a home here with us."

"Dear ladies," said Ben, "'tis a long journey to Yorktown. You could be killed or captured. Believe me, the Brits are brutal. If they win this battle, they would be pleased to drag you aboard one of their prison ships. Those tubs are leaky and full of rats. Too many of my comrades were put in chains there and have not been seen since."

"Mother, won't you please stay?" Elisabeth asked again.

Mama looked down at her swollen hands. The fatigue in her face gave her answer.

Alas, I am the foolhardy one of this family. If anything happens to Willie, I want to be there. "Mother, please do not worry about me. I shall look after Papa, too."

Now, to close this diary and set aside my pen. I am comforted seeing Sally and Johnny asleep by the fire, their thin arms draped over Captain's furry neck. At long last, they shall have their own dog to play with.

And Mama shall finally be able to rest. Her dear friend Mrs. Campbell — Willie's mother — has also decided to stay. Her brick house with the blacksmith stable is just around the corner.

Head of Elk, near the top of Chesapeake Bay

Esther and I are in a tent, rain and wind beating at the flapping sides. Baby Polly is warm between us. We have walked for three days and are now waiting out this nor'easter. There are fewer women than before, about 40 of us. Our group is small enough that a kindly quartermaster said we may board a ship tomorrow morning with some soldiers. Miss Lulu and Mazie are with us.

We have not seen our husbands. At night we pray for them and for General Washington. May God give him wisdom! May God save our country!

Aboard the Birmingham

This schooner is also carrying officers and artillerists, those who man the guns and cannons. All day they have been climbing down into the hold to visit the commissary, which has vittles and a hogshead of rum. I think 'tis the rum they enjoy more than food, because their voices are louder with each passing hour. Their cursing and crude laughter make me nervous. It is odd to think this, but these American boys are no different from those Redcoats so many months ago, when we hid upstairs in a tavern.

We ladies are on deck, sitting in the bow where the wind passes over us. We are grateful to be resting our legs, but are uneasy about these men. If they try to bother us, there is nowhere to run. I am fifteen and married, but I miss my mother!

A lookout up in the mast has just shouted. He can see the sails of a warship, around a bend in the river.

"British cruiser!"

Annapolis, Maryland

An officer has plugged up the hogshead. No more rum. He is calling out orders. Now men are topdeck, balancing on the spars, rolling up sails. I can hear the rumble of chains as our anchors drop overboard.

Our journey by schooner is about to end.

The warship was not our enemy after all, but part of the French fleet. More have come upriver, sails full, their large, white flags snapping in the wind. Such a stirring sight! These ships cast shadows like towering trees. Some are 50 gun, that is, 50 cannons each. Others are 64 gun. We can see these stout, black cannons aimed out over the water.

American vessels are arriving as well. The combined navies will now transport the hundreds of French and Continentals who marched here by land. They shall sail down the Chesapeake Bay, to confront the Redcoats.

I dread that day, but hope for that day. 'Tis a peculiar feeling, to dread and hope for the same thing.

Alas, we ladies must depart the *Birmingham*, to make room for soldiers. We are to climb down a rope ladder over the side, carrying our kettles and bags. A longboat awaits, to row us to shore. I fear tripping on my skirt and falling into the water! Esther is tying baby Polly across her chest so she won't drop her.

How I wish we could stay aboard and drift to Yorktown! But we must rejoin our old friends the oxen, wagons, and horse-drawn cannons. We've been told that a French wagon train will also be traveling with us.

September 21, 1781, Friday

At 3:30 this morning we left Annapolis, guided first by starlight, then by the rising sun. It is now dusk. We are camped on the grounds of a large plantation owned by the Easton brothers. They have been generous with their hay and oats for the animals, and have offered wood for our cooking fires.

Though we ladies have been following behind all the wagons, we can see soldiers from both armies mingle. It seems they are trying to understand one another for there is much hand waving and questioning looks on faces. I like hearing the French speak. Their language sounds pretty, like fast fluttering birds.

A curious complaint: I can no longer sleep on my stomach! Esther said babies change us before they're even born. I believe this is true.

Day four of walking, Georgetown

Another nor'easter. Rain and wind slows us through mud. My feet have not been dry since aboard the schooner. A ferry will take us across the Potomac into Virginia, but many will cross on horseback. Because of the tempest, the river is running high.

We have seen no posters about runaway slaves and I have not asked Miss Lulu if she worries about getting caught. Maybe it's like her honey cake: We'll just keep pretending that all is well.

End of September, 1781

It took two days for our wagons to ford the Potomac. A Frenchman panicked when his horse caught its reins in driftwood, dragging it and him underwater. Both drowned. I think of this man's poor wife or mother far across the ocean. How long before they learn of his fate?

The nib on this quill has split, thus these ink smudges. I must look along the riverbank for a new goose or swan feather.

Next day

We passed a road that turned off to Mount Vernon. An orderly told us that General

Washington just visited there, after having been away for six years. In just one day, he rode the 60 miles from Annapolis, so eager was he to enjoy supper under his own roof with his wife and grandchildren. His aides and Count Rochambeau arrived the following day. Now all have left for Williamsburg. Word is, they are meeting with Admiral de Grasse aboard his flagship *Ville de Paris*.

I have missed being away from Valley Forge these three years, and cannot imagine being away for six. Sometimes I jolt awake in the middle of the night, wondering where I am, thinking, Oh no, I must pack up and move again on the morrow. Oh, for the day that Willie and I shall enjoy supper together under our own roof!

Losing track of days

Sixteen miles today. Ferry across the Occoquan River. My new pen is from a crow.

Next evening

Forded the Rappahannock. Esther carried Polly on her shoulders. Miss Lulu steadied Esther by holding on to her waist. I held on to Miss Lulu with Mazie in between us so she wouldn't be swept downstream. Our dresses dragged as we tried to walk over sunken rocks. The current was fast with whitewater rushing at us.

"Hang on, Mazie, don't let go!" we kept shouting. At ten, she is one of the youngest with us, and I worry about her. I am relieved beyond words that Sally and Johnny are safe in Philadelphia.

Soaking wet all day.

October 7, 1781, Sunday

Yorktown. A sergeant told us we have come 230 miles since Annapolis. In this diary I marked an X for every day: seventeen. We are exhausted. My feet have raw sores, such that I have been limping like a tired dog.

Our tents are on a bluff overlooking the York River. We can see ships patrolling the bay with French and American flags on their masts. Half a mile across the river is another port, Gloucester. An hour ago there were shouts and gunfire. When the smoke cleared I saw three men in red coats sprawled on a dock. At this distance, puddles of blood look black.

Miss Lulu and Esther have gone searching for the quartermaster. We need flour and beef.

Next day

More skirmishes and gunfire. We have learned that the siege began days ago. The French and Continentals marched out of Williamsburg at five o'clock in the morning. In the darkness they began digging trenches to surround Yorktown. They can crouch in these long ditches with muskets. Our cannons have yet to be fired, but are being rolled into place for when General Washington gives the order.

The French fleet has blocked some British warships that were hiding upriver. It seems we are closing in on the enemy, but truly we do not know.

I have not yet seen Willie. The Pennsylvania Brigades are near those of Maryland and

Virginia, but the French are between us. It is dangerous for us to get any closer.

October 9, 1781, Tuesday

All afternoon we have been bombing Yorktown and firing at British ships that are still offshore. Many of them have pulled up their anchors and fled out to sea. A messenger riding between camps told us that General Washington lit the first cannon today, with a new gun brought over from France. The ball burst through an enemy wall, setting it aflame, and was soon followed by dozens more along our line.

The pounding noise, hour after hour, is deafening. Our eyes hurt from the smoke.

I am surprised by this hot weather, and thought it was because of the battle.

"Abby chile, this be the South," Miss Lulu explained. "The South be lots warmer than up in your Yankee land, that's a fact."

Still Tuesday, noon

Early this morning nearly 50 of our heavy artillery were rolled into our siege line, and began their assault. They inflicted such damage that Cornwallis has only been able to return six rounds this past hour.

From up here on the bluff we watched our navies chase some British frigates, puffs of smoke coming from their sides. Our cannonballs splintered their masts, and lit the sails like torches. We could see flames as the vessels slowly tipped onto their sides and filled with water. Before our eyes, four enemy ships were sunk.

October 14, 1781, Sunday

There is no church today. Our bombardment of Yorktown continues.

A horseman told us Cornwallis has lost 60 men since this morning. By the time he rode back through camp, he announced that Cornwallis had just lost another 30. The British general is enraged and panicky.

We ladies are busy. The moment we hang

laundry to dry, it gets soiled from soot and ashes drifting on the breeze. Clouds of smoke block the sunlight. We cough and cough. The best comfort we can offer the men is to carry them water, then they pass the canteens up to those in front of them. At night, our soup is thin. We can see cooking fires across this peninsula — ours and the enemy's. Now more than two weeks into the siege, Yorktown is in ruins. Craters from the explosions are deep enough to bury an ox.

This afternoon a beautiful house was hit by our cannons. The blast killed several British officers dining at a table.

Sunday evening

Our men must go hungry today.

Esther and I prepared a delicious beef stew for them. Moments before we were to give it a final stir, a British cannonball exploded in our fire, scattering the coals and our kettle to the sky. We were too surprised to scream. The other women nearby got ashes in their hair, but were not hurt.

This is not something I shall tell Mama upon my return.

Two days later

This morning we were awakened two hours before sunrise, by the tromping footsteps of soldiers marching or running, we could not tell. Only by daylight did we learn the British were spiking our cannons! This means they damaged them by shoving pieces of iron into the plug holes. A French detachment drove them back to their lines. Fortunately, within six hours our guns were repaired.

Rain and wind make it difficult to keep our fires going.

October 17, 1781, Wednesday

Last evening Cornwallis ordered his troops to evacuate to Gloucester Point. But the storm's high seas, and not enough boats, prevented them from sailing across the river. Even if they could have managed in such darkness, our armies kept launching round after round into their ranks.

How many have been killed, none of us know. Miss Lulu, Esther, and I know one another well enough that we do not need to speak of our worries.

It is still mid-morning, but this has been the heaviest day of bombing. Our troops are manning more than one hundred cannons, firing one after another. Oh, the thunder and smoke! Our heads hurt, it is hard to breathe. Mazie and little Polly no longer cry at the noise, but look at us with pale faces, poor children. I pity our soldiers who are lying in the muddy trenches among all of this, day after day. They are famished, I am certain, because we ourselves are hungry. Rations are pitifully low.

Sudden silence

'Tis not yet noon, but the explosions have stopped. The last one sent up a cloud of black smoke resembling a thundercloud. Its cannonball sunk so deep in the mud, it splattered high above the trees. We felt the ground shake.

Now a flag of truce is being carried through the lines to General Washington. Cornwallis has asked for a chance to parley. He wants to talk.

Cornwallis is going to surrender!

Crowds of people from around the countryside are beginning to gather. We wonder what shall happen next. When and where?

We have learned sad news that one of General Washington's beloved friends, Colonel Alexander Scammel, was wounded and taken prisoner two weeks ago. The British allowed him to be carried by wagon to Williamsburg, but the American surgeons were unable to save him. I remember seeing Colonel Scammel at Headquarters. He was jolly and friendly. During that terrible winter, he was the only one able to make Washington laugh.

Other grim news is about Martha Washington's son, Jacky. He is here in Yorktown, working as an aide to the general. But he is so ill with camp fever, he is unable to eat a morsel of food or even to sip water. The doctors do not expect him to live. Horsemen are racing to Mount Vernon to bring Jacky's wife and children here, and Mrs.

Washington. I can only imagine how this shall devastate the dear lady.

Orderlies are reading lists of American casualties. We are fortunate. Our husbands, and my father, fare well.

October 19, 1781, Friday

Yorktown. From our bluff we looked down upon the field where the enemies were to surrender their weapons. We ladies were surrounded by merchants and villagers, tobacco farmers, fishermen, families with children, and servants, all standing with us to watch. It was the first time I have ever seen so many people be so quiet. There were no shouts or cheers, just a few whispering among themselves.

Soon our soldiers marched proudly onto the field to drums and fifes. The gay military music came to us on the warm sea breeze. The Americans were in an assortment of hunting shirts, brown or white, some wore blue and buff jackets, many had bare feet. They lined one side of the road, the French the other. Officers came on horseback.

General Washington rode up on a great bay horse.

At two o'clock the scarlet-coated British appeared with their Hessian comrades, who were dressed in bright blue and green jackets. Their band played a tune I did not recognize but someone said it was called "The World Turned Upside Down." There were thousands of them, in a line as far as we could see, walking up the road between the French and Americans who stood at attention.

I felt humbled to see women and children following them, perhaps 80 all together, dressed as raggedly as we are.

Then the Royal troops became disorderly! Many of them broke rank, swaggering as if drunk. Instead of laying down their muskets and swords, they threw them in a pile with such force as if to damage them. They stomped on cartridge cases. Drummer boys broke their sticks over a knee and smashed their drums. We could not hear the shouted words, but many appeared to be weeping.

They are being marched to prison camps in Virginia and Pennsylvania. No one knows what will become of the women and children. I suspect

General Washington shall be as gentle with them as he was with Benedict Arnold's wife, Peggy, and her little baby.

October 19, 1781, Friday evening

After the ceremony, we ladies went looking for our loved ones. I found my father first. It had been weeks since I last saw him. He was thin with dark rings under his eyes, but he was beaming with joy.

"Daughter!" he called. "Hooray. You're here! Is your mother all right? Where is she? The children?"

I fell into his embrace. "Oh Papa."

He smiled as I explained about Philadelphia, then said, "Good, good. So Sally finally has a dog to play with."

"Papa, what does all this mean?"

"We are free men," he answered. "We shall make our own laws."

Willie saw me running to him and pulled me into his arms with a kiss. When he noticed my round belly he smiled, then kissed me again. We did not speak, but instead looked out at the bay. Dozens of ships were still anchored offshore, their masts like a forest of bare trees. We could see the large, white flags on the French vessels, and our proud Stars and Stripes.

"Well, Abby. What now?"

Scars on the battlefield were smoldering, but the air was clear. I took a deep breath and looked up at my husband.

"I need a new kettle, Willie. Then let us go home."

Epilogue

After the Battle of Yorktown, Abigail and Willie returned to Philadelphia where he worked as a blacksmith with his father, and where their daughter, Hannah, was born. A few years later they formed a wagon train with their families — the Campbells, Stewarts, Valentines, and the drummer boy Thomas Penny — moving to the Ohio River Valley to homestead.

Willie and Abby had nine children. Hannah became the first female doctor in Philip's County and three sons became lawyers; one moved to Washington City to be President Thomas Jefferson's personal counsel.

In 1804 Johnny Stewart and Thomas Penny joined the Lewis and Clark expedition. After finally reaching the Pacific Ocean, they settled in the West with Shoshoni brides. They were mountain men who guided Teddy Roosevelt on a hunting trip to the Tetons before he became the twenty-sixth president of the United States.

Elisabeth and Ben's daughter, Rose, did not survive infancy, but their sons, Paul and Nathaniel, grew up to be explorers. Paul helped map the Missouri River and became good friends with Daniel Boone. At age thirteen, Nathaniel Valentine ventured to Boston. He signed on as a cabin boy aboard the trading ship *Otter*, which sailed around the Horn into Monterey Bay. In 1796 the *Otter* was the first American vessel to anchor in a California port.

Victor and Miss Lulu farmed the land granted by his former master, and had three children of their own. Mazie and Sally stayed friends, keeping up a written correspondence for decades. Their letters were recently discovered in an attic trunk along with the journals and stories they kept during the Revolutionary War.

Abigail Jane Stewart Campbell died at the age of fifty-seven, after being thrown from her horse during a thunderstorm. That same night, Willie became ill. His daughter Hannah cared for him, but he never recovered. He is buried next to Abby on the family farm.

Life in America
in 1781

Historical Note

The Battle of Yorktown in October of 1781 was a crucial victory for the Americans. British General Cornwallis was forced to surrender his entire army of 8,000 men. Because sailing ships were the only way to travel across the Atlantic Ocean, the news didn't reach Europe until a month later.

The next spring, peace talks began in Paris. Britain agreed to grant America her permanent independence and to withdraw all of its remaining troops from the country. King George III was furious, but America's victory was complete. Before this treaty could go into effect however, France and America needed to agree on all provisions. This was because the Franco-American alliance signed three years earlier stated that those two countries must be in agreement, as must Britain, Spain, and the Netherlands regarding their own territorial and trade disputes.

As a result, these many negotiations delayed the armistice and The Treaty of Paris wasn't ratified until September 3, 1783. Eight years had passed since "the shot heard 'round the world" in Lexington, Massachusetts. The thirteen colonies had finally become a free and independent nation, the United States of America.

Some key points in the Treaty:

- England and America were to "forget all past misunderstandings and differences" and to seek "perpetual peace and harmony."
- Under British rule, ships from the colonies had protection from pirates in the Mediterranean Sea. But now that they'd won their independence, American sailors would have to defend themselves without help from the Royal Navy.
- Prisoners of war on both sides were to be released.
- The British army was to leave behind all property belonging to Americans, including slaves.
- Navigation of the Mississippi River from its source to the ocean would be forever open to citizens of both the United States and Great Britain.
- Under the separate Anglo-Spanish treaty,

England recognized Spanish rule over the colonies in East and West Florida, which the Spaniards had seized during the war. Britain also ceded the islands of Minorca to Spain and Sumatra to the Netherlands, but reclaimed the islands of Saint Kitts and the Bahamas.

After the Treaty of Paris was finally signed, it took the Redcoats three months to evacuate the United States. This meant the war had ended once and for all. Nine days after the British sailed away from American shores, General Washington invited his officers to Fraunces Tavern in New York City. He wanted to bid them farewell. For some moments he was too emotional to speak.

Then, filling his glass with wine, he turned to his men and said, "With a heart full of love and gratitude I now take leave of you. I most devoutly wish that your latter days may be as prosperous and happy as your former ones have been glorious and honorable."

In his memoirs, Colonel Benjamin Tallmadge wrote of that cold December day in 1783: General

Knox "turned to the Commander-in-Chief who, suffused in tears, was incapable of utterance but grasped his hand when they embraced each other in silence. In the same affectionate manner every officer in the room marched up and parted with his general in chief. Such a scene of sorrow and weeping I had never before witnessed and fondly hope I may never be called to witness again."

That afternoon Washington's officers escorted him from the tavern to the nearby waterfront. A barge ferried him across the Hudson River to Paulus Hook (present-day Jersey City), and then he journeyed to Annapolis where the Continental Congress was meeting. Washington resigned his commission as commander in chief, ensuring that the new government would not be a military dictatorship.

Each state, meanwhile, would keep its own militia to protect settlers against Indian attacks and to man forts on the frontier. Now that Americans had gained their independence, they were exploring their new country and moving westward.

.   .   .   .

Four years later — on May 25, 1787 — the Constitutional Convention began deliberating in Philadelphia. The purpose was to revise the Articles of Confederation that had been guiding the new government since declaring its independence from Great Britain in 1776. Because George Washington was the hero of the Revolution and had been the American army's commander in chief, the delegates unanimously elected him to preside over the meetings.

All through the hot summer, representatives from each state debated issues. They borrowed ideas from the British Bill of Rights, which allowed for jury trials and the right to bear arms, prohibited excessive bail, and banned "cruel and unusual punishments" (torture). They wanted to establish a strong central, or *federal*, government that would deal with foreign affairs and defense, and regulate relations between the thirteen states. Above all, they were striving for a government with "checks and balances," unlike countries that were run by a dictator, king, or emperor.

One of the most controversial issues was slavery in the American colonies. Slaves made up about one-fifth of the population, most of them living in the South. Delegates questioned whether they should be counted with the rest of the citizens or be considered taxable property and not entitled to representation. The Three-Fifths Compromise was adopted, wherein each slave would be counted as three-fifths of a person.

Another contentious topic was slave trade and what should be done about it. Already ten states had abolished it, but Georgia and the two Carolinas were still active in buying and selling humans. It was a profitable business for their economies, so these delegates refused to sign the Constitution if the practice were to be outlawed. So yet another compromise was reached: Congress would be able to ban the importation of slaves, but not for another two decades, in 1808.

These debates took three years. Finally, in May of 1790 the thirteen states ratified the new Constitution. Not all were happy with every detail. Benjamin Franklin summed up their views, saying why he would accept the document despite disappointments: "There are several parts of this

Constitution which I do not at present approve, but I am not sure I shall never approve them. . . . Thus I consent . . . to this Constitution because I expect no better, and because I am not sure, that it is not the best." It was a roundabout way of saying, "Let's move forward. It's the best we can do for now."

In the first presidential election of 1789, there was no popular vote. Instead, several candidates were chosen by the electoral college, which was a body of representatives from each state. The electoral college then voted unanimously for George Washington as president, with John Adams coming in second as vice president.

Washington was wistful about coming out of retirement and leaving Mount Vernon, but he felt duty bound to serve his country. He returned to New York City and on the balcony of Federal Hall on Wall Street he was sworn in as the first president of the United States.

Due to the lack of communication and poor roads, many Americans living in the countryside didn't learn of these momentous events for several months.

New York City was the nation's first capital. So it seemed fitting that the popular Fraunces Tavern was used as offices for the Departments of War, Treasury, and Foreign Affairs. President Washington's office was also in lower Manhattan, in the same building as the New York Society Library.

A curious side note about this library: A few months after his inauguration, Washington checked out Volume 12 of the *Commons Debates*—which had transcripts from Britain's House of Commons—as well as *The Law of Nations* by Emer de Vattel. In a huge ledger weighing eighteen pounds, the librarian wrote "President" next to these titles with the date: "October 5, 1789." But whether on purpose or inadvertently, these books were never returned. More than two centuries passed. When employees at Washington's home in Mount Vernon learned of the missing volumes they searched the estate but were unable to find them. They did however locate an identical copy of *The Law of Nations* online for several thousand dollars, and presented it to the New York Society

Library in May of 2010. It was 221 years over-due, but the fine of approximately $300,000 (or 208,877 English pounds) was forgiven.

Washington served two terms as president, finally retiring to Mount Vernon in 1797. He died two years later.

As an aside, some historians believe that if Benjamin Franklin hadn't gone to Paris in 1776, Americans today would probably be speaking with a British accent. He was almost seventy years old at the time, but because of his lively personality and optimism, he befriended the French. He was instrumental in securing supplies and money for the Patriots' cause, and negotiating the Treaty of Paris.

Some interesting facts from around the world during the American Revolution:

- The first children's medical clinic opened in London.
- The first torpedo was invented by Captain David Bushnell, who launched it in New York

Harbor in 1776. He named it after a torpedo fish — also called an electric ray — because it had a fin capable of killing its prey with an electric jolt.

- Captain Bushnell also developed a submarine called the *Turtle*, hoping the Patriots could use it for drilling bombs into the hulls of British warships. It looked like a large barrel with room inside for one man. The "driver" could turn a crank for the propeller, but there was only enough air for him to stay under water for thirty minutes. In calm waters it could travel three miles per hour.
- British astronomer Sir William Herschel discovered the planet Uranus.
- The Stars and Stripes were adopted as the flag for America's Continental Congress.
- Captain James Cook, a British explorer, discovered the Sandwich Islands [Hawaii] on his third voyage to the Pacific. He was killed by islanders in a fight over a stolen boat.
- The first hot air balloon was created by French brothers Montgolfier and launched in 1783.
- In Germany, Beethoven's father presented him

as a six-year-old infant prodigy, when really he was almost eight. His first musical works were printed before he turned thirteen.

- American children enjoyed table games such as dominoes, chess, and draughts [checkers]. They also flew kites, jumped rope, played blindman's bluff, hide-and-seek, marbles, and hopscotch. Girls made dolls from rags and cornhusks.

A drawing of Thompson's Pennsylvania Rifle Battalion of the Continental Army.

TO ALL BRAVE, HEALTHY, ABLE BODIED, AND WELL
DISPOSED YOUNG MEN,
IN THIS NEIGHBOURHOOD, WHO HAVE ANY INCLINATION TO JOIN THE TROOPS,
NOW RAISING UNDER
GENERAL WASHINGTON.
FOR THE DEFENCE OF THE
LIBERTIES AND INDEPENDENCE
OF THE UNITED STATES,
Against the hostile designs of foreign enemies,

TAKE NOTICE,

THAT *Middlesex* Tuesday Wednesday Thursday Friday and Saturday at *Spotswood* in _____ county, attendance will be given by
Lieutenant Reating _____ with his music and recruiting party of _____ company in *Major Stute*
Battalion, of the 11th regiment of infantry, commanded by Lieutenant Colonel Aaron Ogden, for the purpose of receiving the enrollment of
such youth of SPIRIT, as may be willing to enter into this HONOURABLE service.

The ENCOURAGEMENT at this time, to enlist, is truly liberal and generous, namely, a bounty of TWELVE dollars, an annual and fully sufficient
supply of good and handsome clothing, a daily allowance of a large and ample ration of provisions, together with SIXTY dollars a year in GOLD
and SILVER money on account of pay, the whole of which the soldier may lay up for himself and friends, as all articles proper for his subsistance and
comfort are provided by law, without any expence to him.

Those who may favour this recruiting party with their attendance as above, will have an opportunity of hearing and seeing in a more particular
manner, the great advantages which these brave men will have, who shall embrace this opportunity of spending a few happy years in viewing the
different parts of this beautiful continent, in the honourable and truly respectable character of a soldier, after which, he may, if he pleases return
home to his friends, with his pockets FULL of money and his head COVERED with laurels.
GOD SAVE THE UNITED STATES.

*recruitment broadside for the Continental Army, which calls upon "all brave, healthy, able bodied,
and well disposed young men . . ." to join the American fighting forces.*

The old State House in Philadelphia, pictured here, was later called Independence Hall.

The Arch Street ferry in Philadelphia carried passengers across the Delaware River.

A traitor to the Continental Army, Benedict Arnold is shown promising to deliver West Point to the British in this woodcut.

Continental soldiers built winter cabins to weather the terribly harsh winter of 1779–1780 in Morristown, New Jersey.

Dispirited American soldiers huddle around a campfire at Valley Forge.

Martha Washington visiting the Continental soldiers at their encampment at Valley Forge.

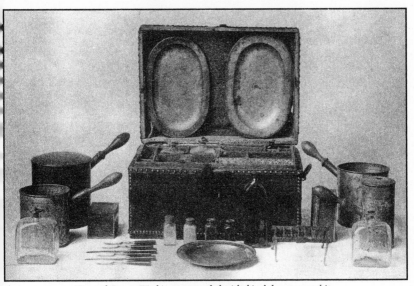

General George Washington traveled with this elaborate mess kit.

An engraving showing the marching band of the Continental Army.

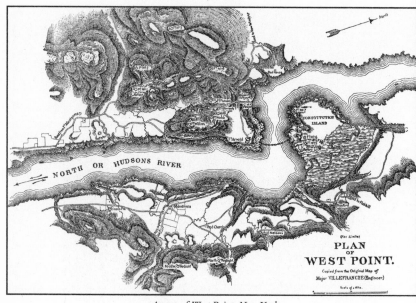

A map of West Point, New York.

A view of West Point, New York, which lies on the western shore of the Hudson River.

In July of 1779, a small band of Continental Army soldiers surprised British troops with a night attack at Stony Point, a key ferry dock and a fortified position of the British Army on the Hudson River near West Point, New York. The Americans took Stony Point in a matter of twenty-five minutes.

An illustration depicting the first meeting between the American General George Washington and the French General Lafayette.

General Washington is introduced to Comte de Rochambeau, one of the commanders of the French forces, which were allied with the Continental Army during the Revolutionary War.

In October 1781, the French and American armies combined forces, under the leadership of General George Washington and Comte de Rochambeau, to attack and eventually defeat the British Army, which was commanded by Lieutenant General Cornwallis, at the Battle of Yorktown in Virginia. This was the last major battle of the Revolutionary War, as Cornwallis's surrender prompted the British government to negotiate an end to the fighting with the Americans.

*The British frigate
Sharon is destroyed
during the Battle of
Yorktown in 1781.*

*The British signal their
surrender to the American
forces during the Battle of
Yorktown.*

General Cornwallis officially surrenders to the American Army following the Battle of Yorktown.

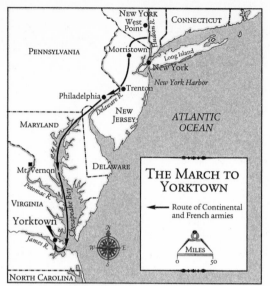

A map showing the path the Continental Army took en route to
Yorktown, Virginia.

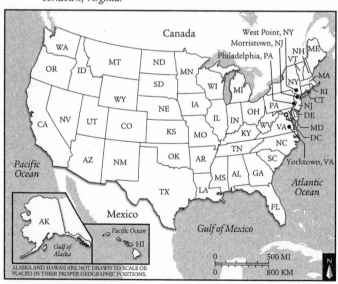

A map of the United States showing West Point, New York; Morristown, New Jersey;
Philadelphia, Pennsylvania; and Yorktown, Virginia.

About the Author

Cannons at Dawn is Kristiana Gregory's sequel to *The Winter of Red Snow*, her first of five Revolutionary War books in the Dear America series. This period of history has always fascinated her.

"Since a child, I've felt a kinship with the Colonial era because several of my ancestors fought in the War of Independence. I walked around the encampment site of Valley Forge many times, and also Jockey Hollow. They're national parks now with clean restrooms, gift shops, and paved parking lots. While standing inside an air-conditioned visitor's center, it's hard to relate to the intense suffering of our soldiers and the camp followers."

Writing *Cannons at Dawn* allowed Ms. Gregory to imagine camp life through the eyes of Abigail Stewart. Abby's diary is a work of fiction, but many of the events and characters are real, including Benedict Arnold, Mrs. Lucy Knox, and her infant Julia Knox.

"It was fun returning Martha Washington to the story, for she did indeed join her husband at every winter encampment, often with her maid Oney. I used a lunar calendar so references to a full moon are historical, as are the blizzards and nor'easters, the reports of the aurora borealis, and the mysterious day of darkness throughout New England.

"One of the best parts about research is exploring historical settings, such as the army encampment sites in Morristown and Valley Forge. In New York City I was enchanted to visit Fraunces Tavern where General Washington said farewell to his officers after the war had ended. This brick tavern built in 1719 is still open for business and now sits among the skyscrapers of lower Manhattan. An editor recently treated me to a very fine lunch there. As I ate pot roast, mashed potatoes, then apple pie, I could just imagine Washington with his officers doing the same that cold December day of 1783."

Ms. Gregory has written more than thirty books for young readers, many in Scholastic's Dear America and Royal Diaries series, including

Across the Wide and Lonesome Prairie and *Cleopatra VII, Daughter of the Nile*; she also created the Prairie River series and the Cabin Creek Mystery series for Scholastic. Her first novel, *Jenny of the Tetons*, which was published by Harcourt, won the SCBWI Golden Kite Award for fiction. *The Winter of Red Snow* and *Cleopatra VII* were made into movies for the HBO Family Channel.

In her spare time Ms. Gregory loves to swim, read, hang out with friends, and walk her golden retrievers, Poppy and Daisy. She and her husband live in Boise, Idaho. Their two sons are all grown up.

Acknowledgments

For help with research and insight into the camp followers, I'm grateful to Carrie Fellows, Administrator of the Morris County Heritage Commission in Morristown, NJ; and for the writings of John U. Reed, specifically, "Female Followers with the Continental Regiments"; and Holly A. Mayer's book, *Belonging to the Army: Camp Followers and Community during the American Revolution*. Another invaluable resource was the 1830 publication by Joseph Plumb Martin: *A Narrative of Some of the Adventures, Dangers and Sufferings of a Revolutionary Soldier, Interspersed with Anecdotes of Incidents That Occurred Within His Own Observation*. A 1995 reprint by Holiday House is titled *Yankee Doodle Boy*.

Above all, I am happily indebted to my editor, Lisa Sandell, and my literary agent, Elizabeth Harding, for their encouragement and support.

Grateful acknowledgment is made for permission to use the following:

Cover portrait by Tim O'Brien.

Cover background: Storming of Stony Point, 1779 © North Wind Picture Archives, Alfred, Maine.

Page 232: Pennsylvania Rifle Battalion, Archive Photos/Getty Images, New York, New York.

Page 233: Recruitment Broadside, Everett Collection/Superstock, Jacksonville, Florida.

Page 234 (top): Old State House in Philadelphia, North Wind Picture Archives, Alfred, Maine.

Page 234 (bottom): Arch Street Ferry in Philadelphia, Topfoto/The Image Works, Woodstock, New York.

Page 235 (top): Benedict Arnold, North Wind Picture Archives, Alfred, Maine.

Page 235 (bottom): Continental soldiers build cabins, Archive Photos/Getty Images, New York, New York.

Page 236 (top): Dispirited American soldiers, North Wind Picture Archives, Alfred, Maine.

Page 236 (bottom): Martha Washington visiting soldiers, ibid.

Page 237 (top): Washington's Mess Kit, Division of Armed Forces, National Museum of American History, Smithsonian Institution, Washington, D.C.

Page 237 (bottom): Continental Army marching band, The Granger Collection, New York, New York.

Page 238 (top): Map of West Point, ibid.

Page 238 (bottom): View of West Point, ibid.

Page 239: Battle of Stony Point, Library of Congress, LC-USZ62-61396.

Page 240 (top): Washington and Lafayette, Library of Congress, LC-USZ62-1409.

Page 240 (bottom): Washington introduced to Comte de Rochambeau, North Wind Picture Archives, Alfred, Maine.

Page 241 (top): Battle of Yorktown, Library of Congress, LC-USZ62-8233.

Page 241 (bottom): Battle of Yorktown, North Wind Picture Archives, Alfred, Maine.

Page 242 (top): British frigate on fire, ibid.

Page 242 (bottom): British signal surrender at Yorktown, ibid.

Page 243: Cornwallis surrenders, Library of Congress, LC-USZ62-5847.

Page 244: Maps by Jim McMahon.

Other books in the Dear America series

DEAR AMERICA
The Diary of Emma Simpson

When Will This
Cruel War Be Over?
Gordonsville, Virginia, 1864

BARRY DENENBERG

DEAR AMERICA
The Diary of Abigail Jane Stewart

The Winter of
Red Snow
Valley Forge, Pennsylvania, 1777

KRISTIANA GREGORY

DEAR AMERICA
The Diary of Patsy, a Freed Girl

I Thought My Soul Would
Rise and Fly
Mars Bluff, South Carolina, 1865

JOYCE HANSEN

DEAR AMERICA
The Diary of Amelia Martin

A Light in the Storm
Fenwick Island, Delaware, 1861

KAREN HESSE

DEAR AMERICA
The Diary of Piper Davis

The Fences Between Us
Seattle, Washington, 1941

KIRBY LARSON

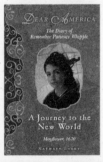

DEAR AMERICA
The Diary of Remember Patience Whipple

A Journey to the
New World
Mayflower, 1620

KATHRYN LASKY

DEAR AMERICA
The Diary of Lydia Amelia Pierce

LIKE THE
WILLOW TREE
Portland, Maine, 1918

LOIS LOWRY

DEAR AMERICA
The Diary of Clotee, a Slave Girl

A Picture of
Freedom
Belmont Plantation, Virginia, 1859

PATRICIA C. McKISSACK

DEAR AMERICA
The Diary of Catharine Carey Logan

Standing in the Light
Delaware Valley, Pennsylvania, 1763

MARY POPE OSBORNE

DEAR AMERICA
The Diary of Margaret Ann Brady

Voyage on
the Great Titanic
RMS Titanic, 1912

ELLEN EMERSON WHITE